Committed

NEW HEIGHTS PUBLISHING
www.suzannefalter.com

Book cover design by Caroline Manchoulis
www.ladylit.com

Book design by Danielle H. Acee
www.authorsassistant.com

ISBN: 978-0-9969981-4-7

Committed

An Oaktown Girls Novel

by

SUZANNE **FALTER**

For Rachel

Chapter One

Sally Pruett stirred and stretched on the made-up couch that was serving as her temporary bed. She sat up and rotated her head on her permanently stiff neck, and winced a little at the pain as she stretched out her legs. She really had to get back to yoga, she thought to herself.

She had to get back to a lot of things.

Sally looked around the living room she was living in and fell back on the couch with a thud. She felt motionless. In fact, her entire life felt motionless. It was as if all the vitality had been sucked right out of it, and she was left swimming in a dirty dishwater sea of bad memories and big regrets.

The obvious could not be avoided. She never should have gotten involved with girlfriend number twelve in the first place. Even going in, Sally realized GF-12 was going to be trouble. A hot-headed Italian-American butch was never going to get along with someone like her—a so-called 'sensitive' who communicated with angels, talked to Goddesses, and secretly read the Tarot. Really, they had no business moving in together at all.

Still, Sally had been hopeful, as she always was in the beginning. At the very least, she'd thought GF-12—or Gina, to call her by her name—would be a little kinder in the end.

But…no. It was the same old story. Once these women understood just what it meant to live with a person whose feet were only marginally parked on this earth, they usually fled. This was just the way it was. Could she help it if she favored butches (the tougher the better) with their muscle shirts, their swagger, and their impossibly sexy mojo? She just did, for better or for worse.

Fact was, Sally was a hopeless case.

Extending one arm out from under the down comforter, she reached for the Goddess cards on her coffee table. Pulling the deck from its box, she shuffled them on her stomach as she thought hard about her situation. She was currently fairly penniless, she had just lost the apartment she'd recently taken with Gina after giving up her own, and the psychic reading business she'd wanted to start for the last five years was still in pieces on the ground.

Now here she was, crashed on a couch in Oakland, California, the land of jacked-up rents, scarce apartments, and fleeing natives. It was hard to say how long Sally could count on her hostesses' largess.

She picked three cards from the deck and slowly turned each one over. The first was Ishtar, Goddess of boundaries, reversed. Which made sense. She thought of their last fight, when Gina had thrown a glass that shattered against the wall. The abrasive sound of smashing glass had rattled through her head for days afterwards. Gina had trampled through her life like there were no boundaries, and Sally was not the better for it.

Sally turned over the next card, the Celtic Goddess Oonagh, with her exhortation to relax and slow down. God bless Oonagh, she thought fondly. She could always be counted on to put in a vote for rest at a time like this. Ostara, the Goddess of fertility and new beginnings, appeared in the final position, indicating that it was time to begin a new life. And it was. Sally fully understood that now.

A fourth card jumped out of the deck, appearing to follow the previous three. This usually meant something important, so Sally eagerly turned over the card. It was Bast, Egyptian Goddess of independence, and the card was reversed.

Sally had never pulled Bast from the deck before, and she stared at it curiously. In no uncertain terms, the card was telling her she needed to cultivate independence. And that independence would ultimately be the source of her strength.

Independence, Sally pondered this for a moment, curiously. When a card was reversed, it usually meant that this was something that was currently missing in her life, or something that required special attention. She sighed. Sure enough, here she was yet again, depending on friends for her basic survival. Sally was, indeed, at a crossroads of her own making.

Curling up once again under the down comforter, she hid her head as a surge of little girl fear poured through her. She needed to grow up—even now, well into adulthood. She needed to put her feet on the ground and get a grip. That was the great lesson of girlfriend number twelve, Sally realized. But how in the hell was she going to do this?

Tenika and Delilah's bedroom door opened, and she heard Tenika pass by on her way to the bathroom. "Hey, sister," Tenika said.

Sally liked that she called a White girl like her 'sister.' It made her feel welcome and appreciated. She didn't know Tenika so well. It was Delilah she'd known far longer, going all the way back to freshman year of college. Yet, Tenika seemed to be the one who was looking out for her now.

"Morning, T," Sally said to Tenika as the bathroom door gently closed. Hugging herself, she said a small prayer.

Help me, Mother, she prayed. *Help me show up in good faith and get the job done—whatever it is. And please help me keep going,* Sally added, as the thought of completely rebuilding her life began to overwhelm her once more. *Help me keep on, no matter what it takes, Mother. Please help me get a grip.*

The Mother Goddess was silent as usual in response, but still Sally felt better. Pulling back the covers, she stepped out of bed.

It was time to begin again. However tentatively.

*

Delilah lay in the half light, replaying the scene that had just unfolded. Through the bedroom wall, she could hear her partner. Tenika was brushing her teeth as if nothing particularly significant had just happened. But then…what did she expect?

She pretty much knew going in what Tenika would say about the idea of getting married.

Even though it was seven freaking years into their relationship, and marriage had been legal in California for several years now. Even though all of their queer friends were slowly but surely getting married, two by two.

Delilah was a marrying woman. That's just who she was. And Tenika knew it. They even agreed on all the important things—children (no), pets (a cat), best groceries (Berkeley Bowl), best weed (Kush), best mayor (Ron Dellums). And living in Oakland (of course). But they didn't agree about getting married.

Tenika just couldn't see it, or at least that's what she'd said in the past. After Delilah gingerly brought up the idea in their after-sex, pre-breakfast reverie, her words seemed to fall into a void. "So when are you going to put a ring on it?" she'd asked as Tenika was purring into her ear.

She could feel the tension as Tenika suddenly stopped. "A ring…like…marriage?" she'd asked, pulling back slightly.

"Well, yeah… I mean…you know," Delilah had flustered, immediately sensing her partner's hesitation. But instead of melting away, she'd held firm. She was so sick of wondering and speculating and longing, and leaving little hints that never got picked up. It was time to come right out and talk about the elephant in the room. "Yes," Delilah finally admitted, knowing full well what the response would be. "I think we should get married, T."

"Oh, baby girl," Tenika began. She looked up apologetically. "We talked about this way back in the beginning. You know I can't. I've told you that."

4

They looked at each other for a moment. "I'm sorry," Tenika said gently. Then she did what she always did at difficult moments. She just stood up and wordlessly walked out of the room, her tall rangy body moving towards some unseeable but important land-mark in the distance.

Once she started moving out the door, Delilah knew the conversation was over. It would be futile to bring it up again.

Rolling over, she buried her face in her pillow and began to weep as silently as possible.

*

Tenika looked at herself in the bathroom mirror appraisingly. She wasn't getting any younger, that was for damn sure.

Striking an angle, she looked at her jaw. Then turning her head the other way, she looked hard to see if she could detect the jowls that threatened to creep in at mid-life, just like they had with her father and Uncle Marcus. And yeah, she was probably just about due for getting glasses to read every last damn thing.

Tenika took a breath and stared at herself. Not only was she getting older, effectively, she'd just ended the relationship with the only woman she'd ever really loved.

What the hell was she doing?

Well, okay, she hadn't ended it-ended it. Just dinged it irrep-arably, perhaps. Or dented it so it would never drive true again, even if the dent got completely hammered out or the bumper got completely replaced. Tenika knew such body work was futile be-cause in the end, you couldn't unsay certain things, and the other person sure as hell couldn't unhear them.

She'd just told Delilah that she was never going to marry her. Like…ever. Tenika did this because she had to. Because it was the honest and right thing to do.

She hated to make Delilah cry. She honestly hated it, and even though she could hear no sound issuing from the bedroom, she was pretty much sure that was what was happening right now. Still…Delilah knew.

Tenika had told her how she felt about marriage when they got together. She could still remember her exact words.

"I'll do anything you want but get married. I just plain old don't believe in it."

The problem was the nature of the beast. How could you commit to legally bind yourself to another person for the rest of your life? It just made no sense to Tenika. People changed. Circumstances changed.

Love changed.

And yet…

Splashing her face with cold water, she paused for a moment and watched the water drip off of her face. Just on the other side of that wall, the woman she loved was hurting because of her words. Because she was too resistant, or maybe too chicken, or too whatever to woman up and do the right thing. But hey, she had to be honest.

Right?

Still, Tenika wavered as she regarded herself, and her thoughts spun in circles. A small muffled sob seeped through the bathroom wall.

What if getting married actually *was* the right thing? Her own parents had married, and then divorced. Then they married, and divorced again. Still neither had the strength to walk away completely. They'd just strung along together for decades, sometimes on and sometimes off, until her mother finally died of cancer.

Her father was still devastated. They'd had other lovers, but in the end, they always came back to each other. Theirs was a love that prevailed in spite of the institution of marriage, and it seemed the truest kind to Tenika.

A knock sounded on the door. It was probably Sally. "Out in a sec," Tenika said.

"Do you want coffee?" she heard Sally ask.

"Oh...nah. I'll get it while I'm out." On this particular morning, she was going to have to slip out the door fast. Even if it was a Saturday and the garage was closed. That's all there was to it.

"Okay," Sally said a little too evenly, as if she was already aware of what was going on.

Tenika heard Sally pad back towards the kitchen. The silence coming from their bedroom was still deafening. Squaring her shoulders, Tenika snapped off the bathroom light and headed back into their room, clearing her throat as she went.

It was time to get dressed and get on with the rest of life.

*

Lizzy hurried after Kate as she moved up the narrow passageway at the Grand Lake Farmer's Market. Even though it was only May, the stalls were laden. In Kate's overstuffed bag were already the makings of many green salads, with a heap of strawberries, a baguette, and a bottle of local kefir. "Honey," Lizzy called. "Do we have any walnuts?"

Kate spun in her direction. "Guess the fruit?" she asked. She was smiling at Lizzy, holding something behind her back.

"Sure," said Lizzy gamely, closing her eyes and opening her mouth. It was a game they played with the fruit samples at the market.

Lizzy felt her girlfriend put something cool and moist in her mouth. She bit down and the piquant-sweet flavor of a pluot filled her mouth. "Plum—wait, no...pluot!" she declared.

Kate nodded with a smile. Taking her hand, Lizzy moved on beside her. As ever, Kate was in charge at the market, but what an *in charge* it was. They stopped before the organic meat stand. "Oh, look...they have lamb stew meat. Some lamb stew would be lovely," she said, her light Irish accent coloring her words. "My mum's lamb stew…" Kate said a bit wistfully. "Honestly, I could cry like a baby sometimes just thinking about it."

Lizzy put her hands in her pocket. "Then get some," she said with a shrug.

Kate gave a little gasp of disapproval. "Lizzy—the price!" she whispered with a head nod. The stew meat was more than $10 a pound. But it was organic, pasture-raised lamb, and probably lovingly massaged with almond oil and read to every night as well.

"Get it—it's okay. I want to try your mom's stew. Come on, we can afford it!" Lizzy exhorted.

Kate shot her a doubtful look. "What?" Lizzy said innocently, as if they hadn't just had a conversation about financial obligations the night before.

"Another time," Kate said lightly, moving on. "Look, there's the falafel man," she continued smoothly.

Lizzy followed along with a grin. Lamb stew or no lamb stew, at times like this, she simply couldn't believe her luck. Even though it had only been two months since they'd gotten together, Lizzy already knew. This was *It*.

Like…seriously *It*.

She'd been around the block more times than she cared to remember, but this time it was completely different. At least, that's what Lizzy told herself. Even if they had been forced to move in together on their second date, after Kate suddenly lost the room she was living in.

And even if Kate was technically an undocumented worker who was finding it nearly impossible to find work. And even if Lizzy was her primary employer now, ever since her previous job with a celebrity race car driver had ended with an abrupt thud.

And even if that very same peevish race car driver could at any time report Kate to ICE.

Aside from that, Kate was everything Lizzy had been looking for all these years. There was an essential knowing she couldn't get around. She felt it in her gut. They knew each other—*really knew each other*—like no one else in her entire life. Not to mention the fact that sex was spectacular, fun, and frequent. The last two months had been entirely heady.

These days, Lizzy wanted to bound through her life putting exclamation marks on everything. Again and again, she'd thanked the gods, the angels, her dead parents and grandparents, and anyone else she could think of who might have sent Kate her way.

Yes, indeed. This was *It* for sure.

"Hey, look at that!" Lizzy burst out, pulling Kate to her side. She slid her hand around her girlfriend's waist, and pointed to the rustic baked goods displayed on a wooden cutting board. "I hear their chocolate macaroons are fantastic. Want one?"

Kate looked at her mischievously. "What are you thinking?" she asked slowly.

"What?" Lizzy feigned innocence, for in that moment she actually wasn't thinking about sex. "It's just a cookie."

More than once their lovemaking had involved some choice ingredients, including chocolate.

"Lizzy...I know just where your mind goes, love," Kate reproached with a smile.

"Kate! It's a cookie!" Lizzy protested, pulling her lover closer and kissing her hair. "Come on, have one with me."

Kate smiled and pulled away a little shyly. "That's fine," she said gently. "You get one and give me a bite."

Kate stepped out of her embrace and busied herself with the olive oil stand next door, as Lizzy bought the cookie. And once again, Lizzy felt that cool breeze of subtle detachment as her girlfriend slipped away. It was just her way, Lizzy told herself. Kate was a realist. She had to keep her feet on the ground, for her position as an upstanding resident of the Bay Area was far more tentative than Lizzy's.

Lizzy had the garage, for one thing, and she was born and raised an American. Meanwhile, Kate, an Irish national, was hanging on to living here by the slenderest of threads. Every day, she woke up expecting to get a knock on the door from Immigration.

No, Lizzy told herself, she needed to give Kate plenty of slack. For nothing less was needed to make this precious union work.

*

Home from the market, Kate bustled around the kitchen, putting things away. She reached into the last of the canvas bags and extracted a paper sack she didn't recognize. Opening it, she glanced in and found the pound of organic lamb they'd passed by earlier. She put it on the kitchen counter.

Lizzy.

Really, she was incorrigible. Immediately, she wondered how much it cost. How were they going to keep to a budget if she kept doing things like this?

Yet, in spite of herself, Kate smiled. Of course, Lizzy ran back and bought the stew meat. She must have done it while she was waiting for Kate when she was buying bread. Closing her eyes for a moment, Kate fought back her tense rush to judgment. She took a deep breath, and then one more.

Lizzy only wanted to make her happy, she told herself. Lizzy was so eager to please, so devoted to Kate, that honestly it threw her. She simply wasn't used to such adoration. Or any at all, really.

Only two months earlier, she'd been living in the house of her former boss, Mindy Rose, a retired race car driver who basically owned Kate. Without Lizzy, she'd still be there, she reminded herself.

Kate took the lamb out of the bag, put it in the refrigerator, and fought the urge to correct her girlfriend. For Lizzy was still technically just her girlfriend—not her partner. Kate was careful never to use the 'P' word around Lizzy.

It was far too soon, for one thing. In Kate's mind, they barely knew each other. And she was looking for her own place—she really was. It's what was prudent, wasn't it? Essential, really.

Every day, Kate dutifully checked the listings on Craig's List. Every day she made calls and stood in lines to view the few listings that were available. She'd even filled out applications for the two possible rental rooms she'd found that she could actually afford, but she had yet to get a call back. Kate supposed she was probably far too honest in listing her employment as 'Freelance Marketing Consultant.'

Lizzy appeared in the kitchen doorway, and arranging herself against the door jamb, crossed her arms. "So?" she asked, a happy look of expectancy on her face.

"I found your little surprise," Kate said a little too tartly.

If this bothered Lizzy, she didn't show it. Instead, she had a look like a cat contemplating a bowl of cream. "And…?"

In spite of herself, Kate gave a small smile. "And…well…you were very, very bad, Lizzy."

"The hell I was," Lizzy protested. Then walking over to Kate, she took her in her arms and gave her a deep kiss. Rising up on her tiptoes to meet her lover, Kate dissolved once more in her arms as her mouth found Lizzy's. This was where they met, again and again. Here and in a million other places, as well. She knew that.

There was really no avoiding it. She appeared to be falling in love with Lizzy. Except when she wasn't.

Perhaps it was just an old habit to resist, Kate thought to herself as they made their way to the bedroom, walking and kissing and undressing at the same time. As they fell onto the bed together in a jumble of arms and legs and writhing bodies, Kate had this final thought…

I'm in this…whether I like it or not. .

*

Undercover SFPD officer Sergeant Frankie Kennedy stepped out of her house and into the Oakland sunshine. It was well past eleven, but it was still early for Frankie. She'd been pulling the night shift lately. But on this particular morning, she wanted to hit the Grand Lake Farmer's Market before she had to report to the station.

Specifically, she was looking for strawberries. And Point Reyes Farmhouse Blue, her favorite cheese.

The sun was already high and the sky was brilliant, which meant it would probably not be foggy in San Francisco. Instead, it was likely to be on the warm side at Golden Gate Park where the festival was being held. Frankie contemplated the hot, cumbersome layers she was forced to wear to conceal her body armor and weapon. Then, as usual, she shrugged it off.

Some things you could do nothing about. Life was like that, right? Unpredictable. Like she never could have predicted that her former partner, Dree, would be dead four months after her cancer diagnosis. Or that she, Frankie, would be the one left behind. Or that now, almost three years later, she'd have sold the sailboat and moved to Oakland with the express intention of dating again.

All of it was entirely weird. Frankie shrugged off her thoughts as she pulled out her car keys. Then she stopped.

Ahead of her was something else she was completely unprepared for. The driver side taillight of her car had been smashed. Frankie sighed and swore lightly. Standing there, she stared at the broken light curiously as she touched its jagged edges. Fine red plastic debris lay around the tire. There were no scrapes or dents or marks on the car to indicate it had been sideswiped.

It was as if someone had taken a rock and just randomly smashed her taillight. Someone, perhaps, who knew somehow that she was an undercover cop.

Frankie shook her head and got into the car, nonplussed. *Whatever.* She'd get it fixed tomorrow.

Starting up her car, Frankie pulled out fast and took off.

Chapter Two

Lizzy turned the doorknob to the Driven Garage and gave it the customary small shove. The door opened to a spill of morning sunlight across Tenika's messenger bag, sprawled on the floor. Lizzy half-expected to be hit by the scent of brewing Café Bustelo, but instead she was met by something altogether different.

Tenika was sitting on the couch in the garage's customer conversation corner with her head in her hands. She looked up miserably as Lizzy approached. It appeared she had been crying.

"What the hell?" Lizzy said walking towards her. "Are you okay?"

Her usually buoyant partner sat back against the couch with a protracted sigh. "Hi," she said. Then she looked at Lizzy. "You got to help me, girlfriend. I screwed up big time."

"What?" Lizzy said, sitting down beside her.

Tenika crossed her arms and stared at the opposite side of the garage. "Over the weekend, I told Delilah I can't marry her."

"Oh Jesus, T. Why the hell'd you go and do that?" Lizzy protested. "You guys are, like, the best lesbian couple in the East Bay. You're solid. Why not just marry her if she wants to?"

Tenika shifted miserably on the couch. "Because I just don't believe in it. We've been over this, Lizzy. Remember?"

Lizzy sighed and turned to her business partner. "So what's happening now?"

"I don't know…I don't know! She's being polite. And cool and distant. I mean—she's incredibly hurt."

"But you love her…"

"Of course, I love her! She's the best thing…" Tenika's voice broke and tears formed in the corners of her eyes.

"But?"

"But…*shit*. I don't know. *I don't know!*" Tenika stood up restlessly. "Come on. Forget about it. I should never have mentioned it," she said, moving off towards the rest of the garage. "We have work to do," she muttered over her shoulder.

"Okay," Lizzy said to no one in particular. Then she followed, aware yet again how supremely lucky she was to be in love with Kate.

*

Half an hour later, Tenika closed the hood on the hybrid she'd silently been working on. "Look," she continued without missing a beat, pulling off her latex gloves. "It's not that I don't love her. I love her for all I'm worth. You know that, Lizzy."

"Mmm-hmm." Lizzy did not look up from the delicate wiring job she was in the middle of.

"I'd follow her anywhere, right? I mean…anywhere."

"Yeah," Lizzy affirmed, giving a small tug with her pliers. A spark flew out, and she drew back. "Shit," she muttered, as she approached the wiring more gingerly.

"But marriage is…like…permanent. So you got to be crazy to get into all of that, right?"

Now Lizzy looked up. "I don't think it's crazy. I'd marry Kate if she asked. Maybe even if she didn't. In fact, I'll probably propose at some point."

Tenika put her hands on her hips. "See? That's just what I'm talking about. You barely know each other, Lizzy. This is Hallmark Cards talk—this isn't reality. Don't forget forever is a helluva long time, sister. And you've known each other for…what…two months?"

"Yeah, yeah. Whatever," Lizzy said into the engine in front of her.

"No! I mean it. You don't have nearly enough information, Lizzy. You're just love drunk," Tenika declared, tossing the gloves in the trash.

"Not such a bad way to be. Anyway, I'm serious." Another small spark issued forth from the wiring system she was working on, and Lizzy cursed softly. Putting down her pliers, she looked at Tenika. "I love her," she said simply. "I'd marry her tomorrow."

"Good morning!"

The two women suddenly stopped and looked up to see Kate advancing on them rapidly, a large bunch of wildflowers in her arms. Tenika glanced over at Lizzy with raised eyebrows. Lizzy, meanwhile, was trying to assess how much Kate had heard her say.

"Look what I just found. Your neighbor let me pick them," Kate continued happily.

"Mrs. Cressida?" Lizzy burst out a little too eagerly. She'd never spoken as much as two words to their elderly neighbor. "Nice work. Anyway, she's *our* neighbor, honey," Lizzy gently corrected with a smile.

"Yes, well…" Kate demurred. "Hello there, T," she said evenly.

"You working here today?" Tenika asked Kate.

"I could," Kate replied. "I need to put these in water. I figured you didn't have a lot of vases in the garage so I brought one," she explained. Then Kate busied herself with arranging the flowers on the table in the conversation corner.

The conversation corner had been Kate's little invention—a gracious, comfortable gathering spot for local lesbians to sip coffee and talk while waiting for repairs.

"Kate's going to take care of a little more customer love today," Lizzy explained. But Tenika lowered her voice to a worried half-whisper. "Lizzy," she insisted, "I've asked you this before, and you need to answer me. What are we going to pay her with? Good intentions?"

"Relax," Lizzy shot back, "we can swing this. It's minor. Anyway, she's working for half her usual rate."

Tenika said nothing. She just shot Lizzy a look.

Meanwhile, Lizzy leaned in to Tenika. "Did she help us save this sorry ass garage or not?"

"She did," Tenika admitted. It was true. Kate's brainstorm two months earlier to offer Valentine's Day lube jobs, and set up what basically amounted to a customer flirtation corner in the garage had been a significant draw. In fact, it had saved them from going out of business just as their rent was massively jacked up. Because of Kate's efforts and ideas, they were back in the black.

"Then keep the faith," Lizzy whispered. Straightening up, she raised her voice. "And believe in love, T. Turns out it's pretty much all we got."

"Whatever," Tenika said with a sigh as she turned back to the Toyota. She should have known better than to spill her worries to the lovesick Lizzy.

It was like getting financial advice from a hardcore gambler.

*

Frankie cruised down San Pablo, eyeing the blue line on the GPS as it led her to the Driven garage. It was Monday, her day off. A good day to get things done. A moment later she pulled up and parked.

"Hey there," came the voice that greeted her as she stepped out of her car, just beyond the open bay doors of the garage.

"Hi," said Frankie, looking up. "You folks fix taillights?" She'd shown up at the garage on the assumption that a woman-owned garage was going to not only give her a better deal, but they'd probably get the job done promptly, and without a lot of attitude. At least that's what their online reviews promised.

"We fix pretty much everything," said a tall, skinny African-American woman walking towards her. Her braids were held back beneath a yellow bandanna. She gave her wire rim glasses a small shove up her nose. "How you doin'?" she said, extending a hand. "I'm Tenika."

"Frankie Kennedy. Got a broken taillight here," she explained. "It's a 2015."

"I see," said the woman, crouching down to inspect the broken light. She stood up. "Let me check what we got in the back. Might have the bulb, but the housing probably has to be ordered." Then she headed off towards the back of the garage and disappeared.

"Hullo there!" another voice said, this one lilting British or maybe it was Irish. It was coming from a pretty, slender woman with long strawberry blond hair. She got up from a laptop at a small table and chairs in the corner. A large bouquet of wildflowers adorned the table, and just beyond it, an inviting, overstuffed couch beckoned. Above her head, a sign identified this as the 'Conversation Corner'.

Frankie felt an unaccustomed pull to sit down on the couch, to sink back and relax in it for five minutes. Maybe there was even some coffee around, she surmised. Then she shook off the thought and continued to stand, assessing the place. She didn't need to move in quite yet.

Now the strawberry blonde approached her. "I'm Kate," she said with a smile.

"Frankie Kennedy." Frankie extended a hand.

"Welcome to Driven, Frankie. Can I get you a bit of tea while you're waiting? Or a little coffee?"

"Actually coffee would be great. Just black." *Sweet*, she thought to herself.

"I can do that," Kate said. She caught Frankie's eye and smiled. "Come in and sit down. This is our special little nest for the customers. Because you know, everyone needs a bit of refuge once in a while." She gestured to the couch as she moved towards a coffee maker.

A moment later, Frankie was trying to not fall asleep on the couch. Her eyes were getting heavier and heavier as she waited for the all-important coffee. This was what eleven hour shifts did for her by the end of her work week. She was flat out exhausted.

Kate appeared now and handed her a steaming mug of black coffee. It was strong and dark, and it smelled fantastic. Then she sat down beside Frankie. Instantly, Frankie began to leap up. But then she caught herself and lowered herself to the all-too-comforting couch cushions once again.

She really needed to stop doing that.

"So Tenika's taking care of you?" Kate asked, and Frankie nodded. "And what are you here for?" she continued.

"Oh, just a broken taillight."

There was another brief silence. *Why couldn't she let go a little? It was her day off, for God's sake. Why not have an actual conversation with this perfectly nice, even attractive woman.* "I don't actually... uh...know how it got broken," she muttered half to herself, feeling a little self-conscious.

Kate smiled, and immediately Frankie felt herself relax a bit. "No matter," Kate continued. "Things happen. We'll get it taken care of." Her tone was supremely reassuring.

"So you work here, too?" Frankie asked, trying to make conversation.

"In a manner of speaking. I'm something of a customer liaison," added Kate, "making sure you have all of your needs met. That sort of thing."

"Well, the coffee's great," noted Frankie a little awkwardly.

Tenika appeared from the bay. "Got your housing on order," she said. "Can you bring the car back tomorrow afternoon? I'll have it fixed up in less than an hour."

"Sure," said Frankie, rising.

"Don't rush out," Kate said a bit more urgently, patting the couch beside her once more. "Unless you're in a hurry."

"Oh...no, actually. I'm not," concluded Frankie, sitting down a little too quickly on the couch. *What was the deal with this chick?*

"I'm Lizzy's girlfriend," Kate explained, as if she were reading Frankie's mind. "That's Lizzy. She and Tenika own the garage." She pointed to a dark-haired woman nearby who was working on an SUV on a lift above her head. Pausing, the woman put her hands on her hips and scowled at the vehicle. Then she glanced in their direction.

Kate gave a little wave and a nod of her head. Frankie watched as Lizzy made her way over to the corner. "Hey," said Lizzy approaching and sticking out her hand in Frankie's direction. Then realizing it was covered with a grimy glove, Lizzy pulled it back, slightly chagrined. "Sorry," she smiled. "I'm Lizzy. Welcome to Driven."

"Frankie Kennedy," Frankie replied. "Nice place. I love this corner thing you've got here." A look of mild adoration crossed Lizzy's face, and she nodded in her girlfriend's direction. "That's all Kate. 100 percent."

"Now, now, stop," Kate insisted. "We did it together."

Frankie realized in that moment she'd never actually been in a garage that made excellent coffee, and then gave you a really nice place to sit and drink it.

But then, it was woman-owned. The co-owner even had a hot girlfriend.

"Are you new to Oakland?" Lizzy asked.

How did she know that? Frankie cleared her throat. "Yeah. But I've been in the Bay for a long time."

"Oh?" Lizzy continued easily, putting her hands in the pockets of her overalls. "Where?"

"Here and there," Frankie replied. She barely knew these people. Now she rose. "Actually, I've got to get on with my day.

But thanks," she said. Draining the coffee, she put the mug on the table. "Nice meeting you both."

"Yep. Glad you made it to Driven," said Lizzy.

"Lovely having a chat," concurred Kate.

Frankie turned away and headed for the door, and behind her, Kate and Lizzy smiled knowingly towards each other. The customer corner was, indeed, working.

Frankie would definitely be back.

*

Delilah picked up the machine and dipped its needles into the tiny plastic pot of yellow ink on the work table beside her. The waiting chest of her client, a tall, bearded man, had been shaven clean, and now he calmly stared at the ceiling. Her job was to delicately shade in the Sierra sunset she'd inked in above the treetops of a redwood forest a few weeks earlier.

Delilah switched on the tattoo machine. Then touching it to his skin, she began the subtle application of the color. Stroke. Then wipe. Stroke. Then wipe. This was her rhythm, the same one she'd been using for nearly 15 years—ever since she'd apprenticed at the Bearded Lady, back when she lived in San Francisco.

She dipped and steered the buzzing machine once more toward her client's arm. Yet now she noticed something different. There was a slight tremble—like there had been all those years ago, when she had worked for Billie. Then it had been nerves, when she had had to keep from throwing up on her first clients because she was so scared.

This appeared to be something else.

Delilah breathed and grounded her feet a little more firmly on the floor. There could be no trembling on this job, that was for damn sure. Stopping, she smiled at her client.

"How are you doing?" she asked, switching off her machine.

He opened his eyes, slightly surprised. "I'm fine," he replied curiously. Delilah used this moment to stop and breathe once again. She had this. Her hand wasn't shaking. It had to be her imagination.

Or maybe it was stress, a residue of her weekend meltdown with Tenika.

Delilah dipped the machine into a slightly darker shade of lavender and switched it on once more. Feathering her touch, she pushed the color across first one petal and then the next, observing her black latex gloved hand as she worked.

No, there was no tremor. It had just been her imagination. Her poor nervous system was just wrecked. That was all. Because... well...

She really couldn't think about this now.

Delilah wiped away the excess ink and the tiny trace of blood that appeared. Dipping once more into a tiny ink pot, she switched on her machine again and applied a small spread of tangerine just above the treetops. This time her hand wandered slightly to the left, and the color seeped dangerously close to the dark green tips of the trees. Gritting her teeth, Delilah dabbed at the ink, grounded her feet on the floor, and breathed. Then she began again on the next petal.

Her client, meanwhile, remained oblivious. Intently, he stared at the ceiling, awaiting the poke of her machine.

She would get through this. Mainly because she had to.

*

Frankie stepped up to the counter for her second cup of the day. "Americano, double," she said. "No room for cream."

She'd already scanned the room, scoping out each person present for possible threats. It was a habit she couldn't seem to drop, even though technically it was her day off and she was supposedly relaxing. Paying for her coffee, Frankie stepped to the side and waited for her espresso to be brewed.

Pulling out her phone, she clicked open her emails. Glancing at her inbox, she felt the accustomed wave of sadness. She had no idea why email made her sad, but then that was grief. Or so said Emily, her grief counselor at the hospice where Dree had died.

Grief was a many headed beast that seemed to show up and stalk you, unannounced, whenever it damn well pleased. Like right now, three full years after Dree's death. Closing her email, Frankie stuck the phone back in her pocket and waited, her hands under her armpits. Reflexively, she looked around.

Suddenly, there was a screech of brakes outside and someone shouted. Instinctively, Frankie raced for the door, barely pausing to open it before barreling outside. A startled spectator at a sidewalk table glanced up as she practically knocked over his table.

Looking wildly around, Frankie saw…nothing. Chagrined, she stopped cold and took a breath. And then another.

At least she hadn't drawn her weapon.

Apparently, a pedestrian had almost been run down by a guy on the sidewalk on an electric scooter. That's all it was.

"Sorry," Frankie said to the man at the table. Then quietly, she opened the door to the café and went back inside.

The demons in her head were real, that much she knew. And with enough therapy or Zen or whatever voodoo was supposed to cure PTSD, she'd be all right eventually. For now, however, she was fucked.

Collecting her Americano, Frankie headed back out the door and did her best to disappear.

*

Delilah looked at herself in the half light of the tattoo studio's bathroom mirror. Holding up her hand in front of her, she examined it curiously. The wide silver ring on her pinkie was moving back and forth ever so slightly. Her hand was smooth, slightly tan, and it was trembling.

She stared at her hand, willing it to stop. It did not stop.

Now Delilah put her hand in her pocket, as if that could steady it, but her hand just kept up its frenetic micro-pulse within the folds of her skirt. Taking her hand out of her pocket, she shook it and looked at it once more. There was no taming this beast.

It will pass, Delilah told herself. That much she'd observed in the four hours since the tremor had begun. This was really no big deal. It was just a little tremble. Even if it did make the second half of the violet tattoo nearly impossible to complete correctly. She was sure it would be gone tomorrow.

Delilah looked at herself in the mirror, and a sudden, un-avoidable wave of fear overtook her. She closed her eyes against the encroachment of tears. She didn't need this right now. She really, really didn't need this.

What was she going to say to Rhonda, the owner of the studio, or all those clients whose tattoos she was expected to complete? How was she going to keep working at all? And if she was sick…well, then she was truly screwed. And without health insurance, no less.

Delilah shut down that train of thought as soon as it began.

And what, if anything, would she tell Tenika?

Would Tenika even care?

Delilah steadily gazed at herself and ignored the knock that sounded on the door behind her. "Someone in there?" she heard a voice ask.

She was fine. She had to be fine. That's all there was to it. She was just having a bad day. Delilah squared herself in the mirror, in-haled deeply, and turned back to work. "I'm done," she said lightly, as she stepped outside.

She was going to be okay because she had to be okay.

It was that simple.

Chapter Three

Mindy Rose poured another glass of pinot noir and looked out her kitchen window. Her pug, Mr. Big, stretched and yawned in her lap. Then he settled back to sleep with a snort. Irritably, she put the dog back on the floor and stood up.

It was entirely too quiet in this house.

Mindy wandered into the living room, clutching her glass, and sat down heavily on the couch. Picking up the remote, she snapped on the TV and stared at it.

No.

No.

No.

No.

A blur of mediocre television programming whizzed by as Mindy found one unsuitable program after another. She switched over to Netflix and buried herself in a ceaseless string of "recommended" program blurbs, none of which appealed to her.

After a while, Mindy snapped off the television and restlessly stood up. The dog now sat in front of her on the floor and looked up at her expectantly. In fact, it was well past his dinner time. And hers, for that matter.

Mindy picked up her now empty wineglass and moved back toward the kitchen, cursing the silence in the house. She needed someone here. A lover. Or a partner.

A girlfriend, even.

But somehow that never really panned out. Pushing open the kitchen door, Mindy stepped inside and turned on the lights. She opened the refrigerator and peered inside. There wasn't much in there. Just a bag of baby kale, a few yogurts, Mr. Big's sautéed lamb, and a bottle of Kate's HP brown sauce in the door.

Mindy grabbed the brown sauce, yanked off the cap, and poured it directly down the kitchen sink drain with a furious shake.

Who gave a shit if it was imported directly from Ireland? Screw Kate, she thought angrily. *Screw her!* Mindy threw the offending bottle into the blue recycling bin with a smash.

Presumably, Kate was now off cavorting happily with her lover—that idiotic garage owner and Mindy's personal nemesis, Lizzy. It didn't help that the Yerba Mate factory she'd tried to push into their space fell through. That had been nothing less than a stroke of brilliance in Mindy's mind. Or so she thought.

But no. The landlord reported back to her that he'd renegotiated their lease. At the end of the day, the Yerba Mate factory went elsewhere, and Driven carried on as if nothing had happened. Not even jacked up rent could force Lizzy and her partner out.

Still, there was hope. Mindy had a new tack in her efforts to force Driven out of business: Deport Kate.

She picked up her purse and her car keys. Then she put them down again and glared out the window once more.

Where was the fucking gratitude? Even if she had fired Kate and basically thrown her out of the house. Even if she had been a so-called "demanding" boss. What was so terrible about being meticulous?

The fact remained that Kate had been good company, without all the complications of being a lover. And she'd been a reliable, uncomplaining assistant for seven years—long enough to get Mindy into the habit of thinking she couldn't get along without Kate, which is why she wanted Kate to live in her house once they'd finally stop touring the racing circuit and moved to Oakland.

Kate's presence at the house pretty much guaranteed Mindy could keep close tabs on her. But somehow, incredibly, she'd still managed to start sleeping with the enemy.

Grabbing her purse again, Mindy moved toward the door. Behind her, Mr. Big let out a whine.

She gave him a silencing look.

"Later," she said firmly. Then Mindy headed out the door, keys in hand.

She needed to go find dinner herself.

*

Lizzy pumped her bike along Shattuck Avenue and thought hard about Kate. Realistically, what else should she be thinking about? After all, it was their two-month anniversary.

She'd bought a nice bottle of cabernet and a bunch of tulips to celebrate. And, she was making a steak for dinner. The last time she bought a steak was…well, who knew? It wasn't customary. That was for damn sure.

Cutting over to Broadway, she stopped at a light and put her foot down to steady her bike. She glanced at the brimming panniers on the back and half-smiled to herself. This was how it should be, Lizzy thought happily. Buying groceries for more than one. Buying flowers. Buying wine. Celebrating life together—because that's what they were doing.

Yet again, she had the thought that had been circulating through her heart for more than a month now. *Kate really was the "big one."*

In Lizzy's mind, whatever problems they had were easily surmountable with one simple move: they'd get married. Marriage ended the ICE threat and Kate's vulnerability to her former boss.

Marriage also ended another threat—that Kate might find a place of her own and move out.

They hadn't talked about marriage, of course, for it did seem too soon to bring it up. But it was just a matter of time, wasn't it? To Lizzy, all of this was possible. Why not? Everything was going so well that each day was just a little more honeyed bliss.

Pulling her bike up to the door of her apartment, Lizzy fished out her keys. Then she paused for a moment. The windows were dark. Pulling out her phone, Lizzy checked the time. It was nearly seven.

Where was Kate?

Lizzy opened the door, wheeled the bike inside and hung it up on its hook in the foyer. Then she stood, hands on hips, contemplating the darkness in the apartment. Kate should have been home by six.

Shrugging off her jacket, Lizzy removed her helmet and began to pull groceries from the panniers. Kate was bound to walk in at any moment.

Carefully extracting the bouquet of pink tulips and balancing them on top of the groceries in her arms, Lizzy sniffed the flowers as she walked toward the kitchen. They smelled of florists mostly, but their centers were inky black. She knew Kate would love them.

She'd be so surprised.

*

Delilah surveyed the assortment of cupcakes in front of her, trying to decide which one was ultimately going to be the best choice. She'd already decided she was going for medicinal chocolate tonight, or perhaps salted caramel, mainly because her brain was so fried with worry. She figured her central nervous system needed it.

The day had ended badly. Her anxiety about her tremor had built throughout the afternoon, and with it, the tremor itself increased until it was nonstop. And noticeable. She'd finally had to stop inking her last client only ten minutes in, pretending she had a sudden migraine.

She had no idea how she was going to hide this from Tenika.

The young woman she'd been working on didn't look convinced when Delilah said she had to stop. And it didn't help that her boss looked at her with the kind of motherly concern that made lying all the more difficult. She had to get out of there at that exact moment—that's all she knew.

A young woman with a nose ring and a beige knit cap handed her the chocolate-dipped peanut butter cupcake and her change. Sitting down at the counter, Delilah daintily cut it in half with her right hand while she steadied her shaking left hand on the plate.

Closing her eyes, Delilah bit into the moist, tender cupcake, and her mouth filled with instant bliss. She felt the creamy peanut butter frosting on her tongue, and the heady dark chocolate of the cake filled her senses. And in that moment, the tremor ceased to exist.

This was where she wanted to be right now. Just alone with no greater reality before her than a chocolate cupcake.

A moment later, Delilah finished the cupcake and sat there, unsure what to do next. She pulled out her phone and studied it. Opening up a browser, she typed into Google the phrase "causes of tremor hand." A short list immediately popped up in the search results.

Delilah's eyes scanned the list intently, and it was daunting.

Alcohol Withdrawal
Liver Failure
Medications
Movement Disorders
Multiple Sclerosis
Poisoning
Toxins
Benign Essential Tremor

Alcohol withdrawal, liver failure, and medications were out. She barely drank, and she didn't take any drugs beyond a daily multivitamin. That left the cheery possibilities of movement disorders, Multiple Sclerosis, poisoning, and toxins. Or something called Benign Essential Tremor. At least that one sounded okay.

Delilah scanned the list again for possibilities. Poisoning seemed highly unlikely. Who would poison her? Toxins, on the other hand, might be possible. There was always the customary wash of the equipment after each tattoo with Madacide FD. Maybe she'd been too casual about handling it. She couldn't remember going near it without a pair of sturdy latex gloves, so even that seemed unlikely.

Once more, Delilah looked at the list. *Movement disorders, Multiple Sclerosis, poisoning, and toxins.* She put the phone away and stared bleakly out at Broadway, feeling completely and utterly alone.

She had to talk to someone about this…but who? Since her parents had both died, Delilah's circle had become smaller and smaller. Her sister was so preoccupied with her twins that they hardly ever talked anymore. And she couldn't exactly bring it up with her friends at the studio. And certainly not with Rhonda, who ran their collective.

Really, the only people she had left were Sally and Tenika… T would most certainly notice—probably the minute she walked in the house.

And what was she going to say? *Yes! I have a tremor! Cool, huh?*

The whole situation was painfully awkward. Especially now that she'd finally broached the M word, and Tenika's lack of marital intentions became abundantly clear. A small sob caught in Delilah's throat as a tear slid down her cheek. She didn't want this. She didn't need this.

She didn't deserve this. Any of it.

Tenika was going to take one look at her and decide she was totally damaged goods. Especially if she had Parkinson's. Or MS. Or a brain tumor, or who knew what? She might as well face the truth, she thought miserably. Now she could just forget about marrying the love of her life once and for all.

Delilah glanced down at her still trembling hand. Any possible lingering, fragile shot at happiness she might have had was just soundly destroyed.

She needed to talk to Sally. And she would.

When, and if, she could even bring herself to talk about it.

*

It was now close to nine, and Lizzy sat dejectedly, staring at the otherwise empty dinner table. She was still waiting for Kate.

The soft candlelight she'd arranged had nearly burned down, and the steak sitting on Kate's plate was stone cold. Beside it was the anniversary card she'd found. On the front was a girl with the same strawberry blonde hair as Kate, swinging on a garden swing. The card sat in its envelope, propped up against the wine bottle.

Next to it, the tulips were arranged in their vase.

Lizzy drained the last of her wine and slowly stood up. Glancing at the table once more, she shook her head and picked up her empty plate. She turned on the faucet, and slowly the kitchen sink began to fill with hot soapy water. Hands on hips, Lizzy surveyed the pans still sitting on the stove, then checked the time again.

Dammit.

Lizzy glanced around the kitchen and felt a stab of dejection. She didn't want to put all of this away as if nothing had happened. This was her special tribute to Kate—her thank you for the best two months she could remember.

But then, she didn't want to waste it either. Setting her jaw, Lizzy dug a glass food storage box out of a drawer and began to put the remaining steak away.

Finally, she stopped herself before she got to Kate's plate. She would leave it just as it was. So then, whenever Kate eventually showed up, she'd know exactly what she'd missed.

There had been no answer to the texts Lizzy had sent—or to the call she'd made. Lizzy scrubbed at her plate and her wineglass, washing them clean. Then she rinsed them and left them to dry.

What the fuck?

It wasn't like Kate was totally unaware that today was a special day. Lizzy had mentioned it casually enough in the last 24 hours. At the time, Kate had just smiled and said nothing.

Lizzy washed her chef's knife and put it on the drainboard thoughtfully. Then she stopped and sighed. Okay…maybe she had actually overreacted. Maybe a two-month anniversary was not that significant to Kate.

Maybe this hadn't been the best two months of Kate's life.

Lizzy sighed and threw down her dishtowel in frustration. "Shit," she muttered. Then she sat down again, unsure what to do next. Not knowing what had happened to Kate tonight was completely perplexing her.

Then there was the other possibility. Something could have happened to Kate.

Of course, this wasn't an entirely new thought. It was one Lizzy had every single time Kate passed through their door to go out into the world. And every single time she found herself saying a little half prayer of protection, because life could be exactly that unfair sometimes.

But what if Kate was lying in a ditch somewhere right now? What if Kate had been attacked? Or gotten lost? What if she'd gone the wrong way and wound up in the middle of a drive-by?

What if Kate had left her?

This thought stopped Lizzy cold, and she jumped to her feet. This possibility hadn't even occurred to her until now.

Nervously, she began to pace, her thoughts racing.

Kate wouldn't leave her, mainly because she couldn't. All her stuff was here for one thing. And she needed Lizzy. Lizzy had put a roof over her head and given her a part-time job. Anyway, other than Lizzy, Kate was utterly alone. For as far as she knew, Kate didn't have any friends. Or anything, really. She was entirely dependent on Lizzy.

Still…

Now Kate's mind played back a small tense disagreement they'd had that morning as they were both heading out the door. Kate had mentioned she might go to look at more apartments, and for once Lizzy had given her some pushback. In fact, her exact words were, "Don't start that again."

Kate had simply dropped the subject and wordlessly sailed out the door ahead of her.

Sitting down once more, Lizzy felt a flush of embarrassment. What the hell was wrong with her? If Kate wanted to find a place to live, she needed to be free to do that. With Lizzy's blessings.

They'd only been dating for two months. And really—they hadn't been dating at all. They'd been living together. *Living together!* It was the ultimate U-Haul. And the very arrangement Tenika had warned her about.

Lizzy could practically hear her friend's cautionary voice in her head: *"This is never going to last, girl."*

Shit shit shit.

Tenika was right, as usual. But of course, Lizzy hadn't listened to her friend. Instead, she'd pushed and cajoled and persuaded, and then she got her reward. A girlfriend who now seemed only marginally committed.

Lizzy remembered her actions with shame. *What was wrong with her anyway?* It was like she'd never had a relationship before.

Pulling out her phone, she considered texting Kate once more. Then Lizzy stopped and put the phone back in her pocket.

She needed to slow down.

Chapter Four

Sally dropped down on the couch beside Tenika and produced the bowl of popcorn sprinkled with brewer's yeast. "Why do I like this so much?" she asked.

Tenika shrugged. "Damned if I know. I think it's nasty."

Resolutely, the two of them sat staring at a program about animals in the wild. A narrator's quasi-British voice droned on. "The wildebeest grazes unknowingly, and then it stops, listening."

The two women watched in silence, transfixed.

The narrator's voice dropped into a reverent hush. "In East Africa, the blue wildebeest is the most abundant big game species …" His voice trailed off. Out of nowhere, a leopard now sprang onto the wildebeest's back, effectively killing it.

As it did, Sally jumped and dug her fingers into Tenika's arm, nearly spilling the popcorn that was in her lap. "Hey!" T shrugged her off.

"Sorry," Sally said, now busily picking up the popcorn around her. She turned to her housemate. "I'm sorry," she repeated. Then she tipped her head. "Hey, T, are you okay?" she asked.

Tenika had tears in her eyes. She rubbed at them with the heel of her hand and an air of annoyance. Then she sniffed hard. "Yeah. Yeah. It's nothing."

"And so death lurks everywhere in the Savannah," the announcer concluded, as the closing titles began to crawl up the screen over soaring orchestral music. Gently, Sally reached over and turned off the TV.

"Where's Delilah?" she asked.

"Don't know," Tenika said tersely.

"Oh." Sally sat back. The silence persisted. "T?" she finally asked.

"What?"

"You okay?"

Tenika looked at her. "Why do you ask?" she said, as if it wasn't glaringly obvious.

Sally gazed back at her. "Because you're crying. And there's a wall of silence in this place, and you're acting weird, and Delilah's not here even though it's Monday night at ten o'clock."

Tenika got up and began to pace. Still she didn't say anything. "T?" Sally finally asked encouragingly.

"You got any weed?" Tenika asked.

Sally shook her head. "I've got some really old CBD gummies, but that's not going to do much beside put you to sleep." She leaned back and looked at her friend. "What's going on?"

Tenika plopped down on the couch beside her friend. "I told her I can't marry her," she admitted. Then she looked at Sally. "Delilah wants to, but…I just can't."

Sally was nonplussed. "Do you love her?"

Tenika looked exasperated. "Of course I love her! I mean, obviously. What's wrong with everyone? Why do I have to marry someone just because I love them?" She turned to Sally, eyes flashing. "I love her, okay?"

Sally just gazed back at her calmly. "But …"

"But nothing! I just don't believe in marriage, and she does, and we're fucked. *Damn!*" Tenika leapt up and began to pace once more. "I explained all of this to her when we got together. It's like this old in-the-bones kind of thing for me. Like…like I wouldn't marry *anybody*, not just Delilah. But she can't get that." Tenika stopped in front of Sally and stared her down. "I don't marry people," she said definitively.

"Okay," Sally responded evenly. "So how's she taking it?"

"Shitty. Extremely shitty. I've texted her three times today, and she barely answers. And she's not here, right? I don't even fucking know where she is."

"Oh, T," Sally sighed. She patted the couch beside her. "Sit down," she said soothingly. They were silent for a moment as Tenika slowly sank down onto the couch beside her friend. Tenika began to cry in earnest. Reaching over, Sally put her arm around her.

"Here." Sally dug out a cotton handkerchief and handed it to her friend. "This is really, really hard. I can feel it. I'm so sorry, T."

"Thanks," Tenika answered gruffly, blowing her nose. Then she closed her eyes. "I'm fucked," she muttered. "Just plain old fucked."

For a moment, Sally was quiet. "I don't think so," she finally said. "At least that's my gut feeling. I think you're just in some kind of transition. I say let it ride. You may wind up being pleasantly surprised."

Tenika looked at her curiously. "Really?" she asked, blowing her nose once more. "How do you know?"

Sally only shrugged, saying nothing.

"It isn't real. My girl is blowing me off, and she's not even home, and who knows where the fuck she is. *That's* real," Tenika said pointedly.

"Point taken, but think of it this way," Sally said, stretching back on the couch. "She's got to go be with what you told her. She has to process it, and it's a lot. You know it is. So give her space, T." She gazed over at Tenika. "If she's meant to be with you ..."

"Oh no, don't give me the fucking butterfly speech," Tenika protested, jumping up to pace once again. "Delilah's not some goddamn butterfly, and I'm not setting her free, okay?"

"But if you do, then she can come back," Sally reasoned.

Tenika turned to her. "So what are you saying?"

"I'm saying, let go and trust your truth. You didn't do the wrong thing, T, and you haven't necessarily broken up. Actually, I say you did the perfect thing—you told her the truth. And she deserves that, right?" Sally paused. "We all do," she added gently. "Wouldn't you want to know if your roles were reversed?"

The two women were silent for a moment. "I guess you're right," Tenika admitted. Then sitting down once more, she located the remote and snapped on the TV once more.

Sally resumed eating her popcorn, and together they watched an old William Holden movie.

"Sally," Tenika said after a moment, "you ever break up with someone even though you didn't want to?"

Sally sighed. "I am so the wrong person to ask about this, T. I'm the dumpee, not the dumper usually. But yeah, I've hurt a few people along the way."

"So how do you live with yourself?"

"Like an old friend, basically," Sally replied. "I mean, it still hurts when I think about it even though I know it was the right thing to do. You can't live a lie—you just can't, T. No matter how hard you try, it's always going to unravel in the end."

Tenika sighed. "Guess so," she said quietly. Then the two of them turned back to William Holden.

"Thanks, sis," Tenika said after a moment.

Wordlessly, Sally patted her friend's knee. "Okay."

*

Lizzy heard Kate's key turn in the door, and she glanced at her watch. It was nearly 10:30, four and a half hours after Kate was due home.

Rising, she put her hands in her pockets and cautioned herself to stay cool. To stay rational, even reasonable. That's what was really needed now.

Really, Lizzy didn't know whether to be furious or just deeply disappointed. She took a long steadying breath. Then she crossed her arms, composing what she was going to say.

"Hello there!" Kate sang as the door swung open and she sailed into the living room. "Have I had a night! I've just..."

Suddenly Kate's voice dropped as she observed Lizzy's demeanor. "I was...uh...well, never mind," she concluded in a small voice, picking up the vibe.

"Uh-oh," Kate continued as she looked around. In the background, she saw the dinner table still set for two, and the flowers Lizzy had brought home. Then she glanced at her watch. "Oh, dear," she said.

"Yep. Oh dear," Lizzy repeated. "Happy two month anniversary."

"Oh, no. No, no, no..." Kate glanced at her watch one more time. "It is, isn't it?" she asked, looking up at Lizzy. There was a beat of silence. Then Kate spoke up in a small voice. "You did say something about this, this morning, didn't you?"

Lizzy shrugged. "It's okay. There'll probably be a three-month anniversary. Hopefully."

"Oh, Lizzy. Look, I'm sorry. I got busy looking at apartments, and I..."

Again she stopped, aware that Lizzy was now looking at her intently. "You're telling me you blew off our anniversary dinner to go find *another place to live?*"

Kate took a deep breath. "Come here," she said, patting the couch beside her as she sat down. Instead, Lizzy lowered herself onto the chair beside the couch, fearing the worst. Then sitting back, she tipped her chin up, waiting expectantly for what her girlfriend would say. Lizzy folded her arms across her chest. She was now in no mood for sympathetic talks.

"Okay," Kate began. "Let me try to explain this again. The thing is..."

Lizzy cut her off. "Don't bother. You need to go live some-where else, go ahead." Lizzy took a deep breath, cautioning herself once more to keep her cool.

Kate sat up a little straighter. "It's not that I *want* to," she insisted. Lizzy said nothing. Instead, she just looked at her.

"Look, it's just that I'm still recovering from the whole thing with Mindy, and I just think if we're really going to be...you know...committed..."

Lizzy leveled her with a look. "Committed? Like that's even in question?"

Kate reached over for Lizzy's hand, but Lizzy pulled it away, unwilling. She glared at Kate, uncomprehending. "Kate, I've given you everything I've got."

"I know, I know—and I'm profoundly grateful!"

"But..."

"But nothing!" Kate stood up and began to pace. "I just..." She hesitated, her words breaking. She spun around and faced Lizzy now. "The thing is I saw a perfect apartment tonight, and I put my name in for it."

"So you are moving out." Lizzy's words landed flat.

"No! Not definitely—who knows if I'll get it? I'm barely em-ployed for Lord's sweet sake." Kate's voice softened. "But I am trying to get my own place."

At this news, Lizzy sat back in her chair and stared ahead dejectedly. "So fuck me for trying."

Kate crouched down in front of her lover, looking her squarely in the face. "No—*no!* That is not what I mean at all. I'm just try-ing to get some space, Lizzy. I need it after everything I've been through. If there's to be any chance for us at all, I have to find a place of my own. But only just for a while."

Urgently, she continued to look at Lizzy. Lizzy just stared back at her, unmoved. "Look," Kate continued, "I love you, Lizzy. There—I've said it. I do love you."

A small smile passed over Lizzy's face, and she lowered her head a little shyly. Now Lizzy studied her jeans. She'd resisted saying those words to Kate, though she'd been moved to many times. Somehow restraint had managed to assert itself here. She glanced up at Kate. "Do you really mean that?"

Kate nodded, tightening her grip on Lizzy's hands. "I do. And I am profusely sorry I missed our two-month anniversary. I feel like a right idiot."

"Yeah, you are," Lizzy agreed a little more easily. "Especially because you missed some fabulous tri-tip in red wine sauce." Kate laughed, and then Lizzy gave a reluctant chuckle. "Come here," Lizzy said pulling Kate towards her. Their foreheads touched, and once more they dropped into their intimate bubble.

"Lizzy, you know I'm grateful. You've given me so much… and I do love you. We've just been dealt a hard hand," Kate continued in a low voice. "Moving in so quickly. It kills relationships. You know it does."

Lizzy let out a low sigh. "Yeah, I know. But you've got to admit, Kate. It's been kind of perfect."

"And I'm grateful, like I said," Kate said. "But it's not real. Not yet." She pulled back and looked at her lover. "I don't want to live with you because it's easy, Lizzy. I want to live with you because it's right. And it's the right time."

"Yeah," Lizzy said. Then she sighed. "Okay." She stood up, and putting her hands on her hips, she looked at Kate for a moment. "You sure you're not breaking up with me?"

"Heavens, no!" Kate asserted. "Not in the least." Then stretching up on her tiptoes, she moved in for a kiss. Lizzy pulled Kate up to her and kissed her deeply, feeling Kate's body surrender to her own.

Pulling back, Lizzy looked at her lover tenderly. She swept her fingers gently across Kate's forehead, brushing the hair lightly from her face. "Whether you live here or not, Kate, I've got your back," she told her. "Don't ever forget that, okay?"

Kate beamed back her acceptance. "Okay," she replied, feeling the rightness of the moment. "And I have yours, Lizzy. It may not always look like it, but I truly do." They kissed once more.

"Thank you for understanding," Kate said.

Lizzy nodded, and their kisses continued as they stood there, feeling their connection. Their rightness.

Finally, the two of them sat down on the couch together, fingers interlaced. "I got a pretty nice bottle of wine in there," Lizzy said. "You want some?"

"In a minute," Kate replied. "First, I want to float an idea past you."

Lizzy looked sidelong at Kate. "I'm listening."

"You remember Frankie?"

Lizzy paused for a moment in thought. "The broken taillight this morning?"

"Exactly," Kate nodded. "What about her and Sally?"

"What—we're setting up blind dates now?"

Kate smiled. "I think it could work."

Lizzy looked at her uncertainly. "How do you know Frankie's even single?"

"Oh, she is," Kate declared. "Trust me on this." Now Lizzy stole a look at Kate and drank in the look of delight that had washed across her face. "I just have a feeling…" she continued. "And if it's not Sally, perhaps someone else…"

"Better ask Sally if she even wants to be fixed up."

"She does. Even if she doesn't know it yet. But yes, of course I'll broach the subject gently."

Pulling Kate close to her, Lizzy gazed up at the ceiling and laughed. "Driven, the Woman-Owned Garage and Dating Service," she spelled out in the air in front of her. "You never stop, do you?"

"Could be fabulous for business," Kate noted.

"Well, it certainly worked for me," Lizzy acknowledged. Then taking Kate's hand, she kissed it and held it to her chest.

She truly didn't want to let go.

*

Mindy peered at the screen of her laptop that glowed brightly in the darkened gloom of her kitchen. She'd been at it for hours, barely even noticing that night had fallen. The dinner hour had come and gone, and only Mr. Big had been fed.

Really, she'd done little more than refill the pinot gris several times. Mindy hadn't even stopped to turn on the lights. The subject of her obsession was Kate.

Katherine 'Kate' Morahan Mindy typed into the field for *Name of Deportee.* Then she typed *Ireland* under *Country of Birth*, and moved on to the field for *Nationality. Irish*, she wrote and then left the field for *City or County* blank.

Mindy stopped and studied her work. Pausing, she drained the rest of her wine glass. Padding over to the refrigerator, she woozily pulled it open, weaving slightly. Somehow the bottle was empty.

"Crap," she muttered to herself, pulling the empty bottle out of the refrigerator. There had to be another one around somewhere.

Mindy had just spent the last three hours diving deeply into the world of Kate and Lizzy and Driven. It wasn't hard to do. For one thing, there was a vast social media web around the two women. Lizzy had chronicled their relationship in detail on Facebook, Twitter, and Instagram, for Lizzy was one of those people who posted everything from her plate of dinner to her mismatched socks.

Mindy also noticed that Kate's last name was never used; nor had Kate taken up a single social media account for herself. But then, that was life when you were an "illegal." *You did your best to hide in plain sight,* Mindy seethed.

Mindy wasn't jealous. No, not at all. She and Kate had no particular chemistry, and there was never even a thought they might become lovers. No, instead she was just plain furious. Nobody left Mindy Rose behind in a trail of dust. Especially not one of her employees.

It all seemed rather pathetic, this so-called love affair of Kate's. In the past few hours, Mindy had read all about their weekend getaway to the Sierras, staying in some god-awful Airbnb, and their day trip to Monterey to see the whales. *Fucking whales,* she thought grimly. Kate and Lizzy were hitting all the Bay Area high notes. A trip out to Alcatraz was undoubtedly next.

So now, she'd simply report Kate, mainly because she could. The new ICE website made it easy to file a so-called *Confidential Report of Undocumented Worker.* Mindy didn't even have to worry about being fined by Customs and Border Protection for hiring an illegal. The fine was all of $375. Not even a wrist slap for someone like her.

Well worth it, she thought to herself as she sat down once more with the open form. Typing in the darkness, Mindy pressed on to the field for *Address.* She paused briefly. Then throwing caution to the wind, she typed in *3257 San Pablo Avenue, Oakland, CA.*

It was the address for Driven.

She didn't know for a fact that Kate was working at Driven, but she might as well be. She'd clearly helped Lizzy up her marketing game, and who knew what else she was doing for the competition. Anyway, if ICE showed up at the Driven Garage, it would be enough to scare the hell out of all of them. And that would be highly satisfying.

A moment later, the form was complete. Pausing to enjoy the supreme satisfaction of turning in Kate to ICE, Mindy smiled darkly at what she was about to do. Then she clicked the red *Submit* button.

Sitting back, she lifted her empty wine glass, attempting to drain the final drops of wine.

If Kate was going to throw away seven years of mentoring— of *friendship*, for fuck's sake—then she could damn well suffer. Because nobody pushed around Mindy Rose.

Nobody.

*

Delilah stretched and yawned as the final credits rolled at the Grand Lake Theater. Then she just sat there, waiting in the dark. Her eyes traveled up and down the elaborate walls of the ornate old theater, taking in nuances of the arches festooned with cherubs and the gilded crown-topped proscenium.

Really, she couldn't have cared less about the movie, a super-hero picture with the usual explosions and special effects. Nor did she care about the theater. She was there specifically to kill time, figuring that if she waited long enough, Tenika would be asleep when she got home.

Eventually, Delilah rose and headed for the exit, meandering past the attendants sweeping popcorn. By the time she reached the big marquee out front, the last of the crowd had drifted away.

Now where should she go?

Delilah looked at her watch and sighed. There was no place to go other than home. That was the sad truth of it. At least she could squeeze another fifteen minutes out of the ride home. Unlocking her bike from the pole in front of the theater, she put a headlamp on her helmet and tucked the edges of her skirt up around her as she climbed on. Setting off along MacArthur, she headed for their house in Bella Vista.

Pumping up the side street next to 580, Delilah tried not to think. Let this ride be like a Zen meditation, she decided. She would just focus on her pedals moving around, her breath becoming harder. Her would-be wife becoming harder.

Her life becoming harder.

Shaking off her thoughts as she crested the hill, she rode on into the dark night. She might as well just prepare herself to tell Tenika what was happening because there was no avoiding it. If she had a serious illness, she had a serious illness. No matter how hard she tried, she could not get around that fact. And maybe it was nothing.

Maybe it was nothing. God, she was tired of that thought. It held as little weight as a feather on a breeze. This was exactly the moment when shit like this always happened to people, she thought grimly. Not to her, per se, but to others, for sure.

Although having your marriage proposal rejected certainly added an especially dark turn.

No, Delilah had never had an actual medical emergency. Really, she'd been strangely healthy all her life, except for the occasional headache. Which is exactly what made this such an uncool conversation at this exact moment.

A few moments later, she sailed down 13th Avenue. As soon as she could see the apartment window, her apprehension heightened. The living room light was on, which meant Sally was awake at the very least. And very possibly Tenika, too.

God, she didn't want to do this.

A moment later, Delilah turned her key in the door. She could hear someone talking in low voices.

"Hello?" she asked tentatively, but no one returned her greeting. Sally had fallen asleep on the couch, and Tenika was nowhere to be seen. An old movie on the TV droned on in the background. Sally now stirred slightly and looked at her.

"Did I fall asleep?" she asked with a yawn.

"Yeah…good night," said Delilah, creeping towards the bedroom. *Saved for one more night*, she thought to herself.

She wondered how long this could go on.

Chapter Five

Frankie walked into Driven and looked around. She'd already found her car parked outside, and the broken taillight apparently restored. Now the two owners were busily conferring before the open hood on a pickup truck.

"Hello, Frankie!" Kate's voice rang out from the counter. "We're all ready for you."

As she said this, Frankie's eye traveled to the conversation corner where an attractive blonde was putting together a jigsaw puzzle. For a millisecond, Frankie felt an instant pull in that direction, but then she inhaled and steadied herself. One attractive blonde quietly minding her own business did not mean it was time to make a play.

Even if she *was* sitting in the conversation corner and working on a puzzle, alluringly alone.

Frankie surmised the tiny red Cooper Mini parked outside must be hers. This woman definitely didn't seem like the pickup truck type.

Now the blonde looked up and smiled directly at Frankie. She had lovely blue eyes. Frankie felt a rosy blush move across her face, and she turned away, eager to get on with business. "Glad to hear it," she said to Kate.

"Lizzy will be right with you," Kate added. "Do you have a moment to sit and relax on the couch? I just made a pot of coffee."

Suddenly, Frankie was being sucked right into the conversation corner. In fact, her feet couldn't carry her fast enough. "I'd love a cup," she said over her shoulder. She was now making a beeline for the blonde.

It seemed too forward to sit down and join her at her puzzling, so instead, Frankie sat on the loveseat. The woman looked up and smiled. "Waiting for your car?" she asked. Her eyes returned to the puzzle pieces. Picking one up, she deftly placed it in its correct position.

"Yeah. Broken taillight," Frankie said.

"That sounds easy." The blonde sat back and sighed. "I don't know what the problem is with mine," she said. "They've been pouring over it for half an hour. Something's up with the supercharger. Once you hit 4200 RPMs, you hit a brick wall, and it won't upshift. It's an engine de-rate, basically." Her voice trailed off.

"Oh. Yeah," Frankie mumbled. She had no idea what the woman was talking about. This was not at all what she expected.

"I'm Tasha," the blonde said. Frankie took her in for a moment. "I've got the truck over there," she added. Tasha was tall and athletic-looking, and her white sleeveless top set off a beach tan and sinewy arms. Her white blonde hair topped a face glowing with who knew what. Vitamins, maybe? She was like a gleaming poster girl for the healthy Californian. Frankie studied her curiously.

"I'm Frankie," she said.

"Nice to meet you," said Tasha, returning to her puzzle once again. "Come here often?" she asked with a laugh.

This woman probably had at least six inches on her. Or so she guessed. She realized she was starting to get nervous. "I try not to," she joked. Statuesque women had never stopped Frankie before.

"Join me?" Tasha asked, indicating the chair across from her. Frankie rose, zombie-like, and found her way immediately to the chair on the other side of the table. Silently, Frankie looked at the puzzle pieces now arrayed in front of her.

"So what keeps you busy these days?" Tasha asked after a moment.

Frankie took a sharp inhale. "Well, not this," she admitted. "Haven't done one of these things in a long time." The puzzle pieces swam in front of her as she tried to make sense of anything she was looking at.

Silence descended between the two women, and Frankie's palms began to sweat. Tasha was undeniably a hottie. There was no getting around it.

"How about you?" Frankie asked after a moment.

"Oh, the usual," Tasha said without looking up. Neatly she put the final piece in the frame she'd been quietly assembling. "There," she said with satisfaction. She flashed Frankie a dazzling smile.

"And what's the usual?" Frankie asked.

"I'm a barista," Tasha said with a smile. Instantly, the detective in Frankie knew this was wrong. There was no way this woman—in her expensive sportswear hoodie with an arm loaded with gold bangles—was a barista.

Frankie glanced over at Tasha's truck. For one thing, it had to be a V8 engine. It appeared to be brand new. What barista drives a top-of-the-line pickup?

"Really," said Frankie, revealing nothing. Now she was curious. She cleared her throat. "You're pretty good at this," she said. Indicating the puzzle.

Tasha focused her blue eyes on Frankie. "I live alone," she said. "I've got plenty of time on my hands."

Frankie could feel Tasha's remark all the way down to her vulva. "Me, too," she replied, never breaking Tasha's stare. The two women smiled at each other.

Now Tasha returned to the puzzle. "What do you do here in Oakland?"

This was always the moment when things got interesting. "This and that," Frankie replied. Experience had proven that if she revealed her profession too soon, it could be a major buzzkill. Or it made the other woman unnecessarily nervous. It was amazing how fast people became model citizens the minute they realized an officer was in their midst.

On the other hand, sometimes it moved things right along.

"Hey, Frankie!" Lizzie now joined them, hand extended, and Frankie rose. "Got your taillight all set. Sorry to keep you waiting." Lizzie paused. "I see you two met. Great!"

"Yeah, Tasha was just telling me about her supercharger. Sounds tricky." Frankie drained the rest of her coffee in a quick gulp.

"Let me ring you up," Lizzy said, heading for the register, but Frankie did not follow. Instead she turned back towards Tasha. Leaning in, she drew just close enough to be provocative. Tasha looked up from her puzzle, and for the slightest instant, she held Frankie's gaze.

Frankie could feel the other woman's power. This was most certainly not some barista. "Lovely to meet you," Frankie said, gazing into her eyes.

"Nice to meet you, too," Tasha said. She held Frankie's gaze. "Would you like to go out some time?"

Frankie smiled. "I'd love to," she said. Within a moment, she walked away with Tasha's information in her phone.

Well, that was easy, Frankie thought, as she headed for the counter.

Maybe a little too easy.

*

"Well, was I right?" Kate asked. She folded her arms as she leaned back against the counter. Then she looked at Lizzy and Tenika with a smile of supreme satisfaction. Frankie and Tasha were now safely gone, their car issues handled for the moment. "It appears Frankie is, indeed, single."

"Okay! Okay!" Tenika shrugged as she peeled off the purple latex gloves and threw them in the trash. She wiped the perspiration from her brow. "Yes, the conversation corner was a good idea, I guess."

"You guess?" Lizzy said. "Frankie and that pickup truck lady were…like…insta-connect!"

"My point exactly," said Kate. "All they have to do is sit back, relax, do a little puzzling. If they're women, they'll talk. And if they're single lesbians and there's any kind of chance, they'll connect. They have to."

Tenika looked askance. "But, Kate, please. Let me play devil's advocate here. How can you be so sure something's going to happen with those two?"

Kate stood up abruptly. "Digit exchange!" she said. "I saw it with my own eyes. Those two women had their phones out, and numbers were given. They *will* be going on a date, Tenika. I guarantee it."

Tenika and Lizzy looked at each other, and Lizzy shrugged. "If you say so," Tenika said, turning to the next vehicle on her list. "I'm still not so sure about this whole damn thing."

Kate turned to Lizzy with a sparkle in her eye. "You know, if it doesn't work with Tasha, I'm still thinking Sally might be a candidate for Frankie."

Tenika stopped and whirled around. "Wait—our Sally? The Sally who's sleeping on our couch? Kate, I mean, come on. She just broke up with someone!"

"Never too soon for love," Kate replied.

Lizzy stuck her hands in her pockets. "Honey, I don't know about this."

Now Kate opened up the appointment book and picked up the phone. "You two are supposed to worry about the repairs while I do the marketing, right?" she asked.

"Right," Lizzy agreed reluctantly.

Kate smiled at her lover. "Then let me do my job, sweetie."

Lizzy and Tenika just looked at each other and shook their heads.

*

Sally dunked the tea bag into the steaming water and watched the swirls of tea release into the cup. Slowly, she picked up the small tag attached to the Yogi Tea bag and read it.

Whatever you are, you are. Be proud of it.

She sighed. This was clearly yet another God shot, but then that's how life had been lately—a fairly nonstop stream of unexpected affirmation.

No, she wasn't supposed to be mired in yet another toxic high drama relationship. And no, she wasn't supposed to spend one more minute sitting in some soul-sucking office, answering phones and pretending she belonged there. When it came right down to it, Sally was no temp. She'd known this for years.

The evidence was clear. All of her efforts to find temp work on Craig's List, this time at least, had consistently failed. Craig's List had always been her fallback position when her Reiki services failed to elicit calls. But this time, there hadn't been a nibble of any kind. The desert seemed to spread out in every direction. And it was mighty dry.

Honestly, Sally had no idea what was wrong. She'd only been out of commission for six months. That was hardly any time at all in the grand scheme of things. The problem, really, was Yelp! When she searched for *Reiki Healing*, her name no longer appeared. It was as if the twelve five-star reviews she had gotten over the last few years had simply ceased to exist. She couldn't even find her name on a search.

But then, this is how life was when you were being nudged in a certain direction. Strange, inexplicable things happened. Technology went awry. Sources of income dried up.

Sally took a sip of her tea. She had no idea what to do next.

The tea soothed her as she sat there in the mid-afternoon sunlight of Tenika and Delilah's kitchen. Something had to shift soon, that was for sure.

Sally reached into her pocket and pulled out the piece of rose quartz she'd been carrying with her every day lately. She set it down on the kitchen table in front of her. It was warm from being nestled against her body, and its gentle pink essence seemed to have a rosy glow as it sat in a shaft of sunlight. "Like a bubble bath for the emotions," her teacher had told her.

As she sat with the stone doing absolutely nothing but being, a thought came to her. Really, it was more of an awareness. The shuffling in of an entirely new train of thought from nowhere, although Sally knew where it was from, of course. It was just a bit more channeled gristle to chew on from her guides.

Oh, those busy guides, she thought with a smile.

There was a place for her work. She simply hadn't found it yet. Taking another sip of tea, Sally exhaled and found herself smiling. Sooner or later, all will be well.

She was counting on it.

*

Lester lay down at the table and looked at the ceiling. His boyfriend, Randy, sat by his side holding his hand. It was time for phase three: the delicate application of color to the violet petals Delilah had tattooed across his forearm a month earlier.

She looked at the colors laid out before her on the side table. They were lovely inks, in various shades of periwinkle and lavender. Usually, she couldn't wait to dip her machine and get going. Just seeing the color fill the petals—each one edging up perfectly beside the next—always filled her with a profound, tidy sense of satisfaction. It was her favorite part of being a tattoo artist.

But today, Delilah was filled with a quiet dread. Only half an hour earlier, she'd been in the bathroom, silently crying after realizing she could no longer tie needles together. Her tremor had taken over even that simple activity.

But coloring larger more general shapes like petals—that had to be easier, or so she imagined. Delilah would only find out by trying.

Steadying herself with a calming breath, she pulled on her black latex gloves. Then she inserted the machine into its plastic sheath. Delilah looked at Lester. "All ready?" she asked.

Lester nodded and looked at his boyfriend for reassurance. The boyfriend squeezed his hand. "Go for it," he said.

Planting her feet firmly on the floor, Delilah grounded herself and commanded her hand not to shake. Then slowly, Delilah dipped the needle in the first pot of ink. Swallowing hard, she switched on the machine, and bending over her client, she touched it to the correct spot on his forearm.

The color inserted itself neatly in place, and immediately she swabbed at it with a tissue, mopping up any excess blood. So far, so good. Delilah began to move back and forth between the pots of ink and the waiting canvas of Lester's tattoo. One petal filled in perfectly, then two. Then five and six. Her shoulder and her neck began to relax slightly.

I've got this, Delilah thought as she proceeded.

It was on the seventh violet petal that everything changed. Her hand now slipped slightly to the right, sending a perceptible smudge of ink just beyond the gray outline of the flower. She stopped and blotted. Then she wiped again, as if a tissue was enough to remove the errant smudge of ink now embedded in Lester's skin.

But no, it couldn't be removed. The mistake was permanent.

A wave of anxiety moved through Delilah, and she turned off her machine and set it down. Lester looked over at her curiously.

"I'll be right back," she said, peeling off her gloves. The two men looked at each other and watched her head back to the ladies' room.

Once again, Delilah confronted herself in the mirror, taking a deep breath. Once more, she breathed, willing herself not to cry. The truth was now sinking in.

I can't do this anymore. I can't do this. The words kept repeating over and over in her mind.

She would have to go tell her client.

*

"What are you doing home?" Sally rose from the kitchen table and moved towards Delilah as she came into the kitchen. "Don't you have work?"

Wearily, Delilah put her messenger bag on the floor and sat down. "You'd think I would, right?" was all she said.

The two women were silent. Slowly, one tear, and then another, slid down Delilah's rose-tinted cheek. Sally reached out her hand. "What is it? What happened?"

Still her friend could not answer. Instead, she continued to cry in earnest, until small black rivulets of washed-away mascara poured down her cheeks. Sally sat back and watched her for a moment. Then she went off to find a box of tissues.

"Here," she said, offering them when she returned. Delilah took a handful and blew her nose. Sally patted the chair beside her, and Delilah willingly moved next to her.

"Can I talk to you?" Delilah asked in a small voice.

Sally leaned in. "What? Of course, you can talk to me. *Please* talk to me. What's going on?"

Still Delilah was unable to begin. Instead, she focused on Sally's empty teacup and kept crying. "Is this about you and Tenika?" Sally finally asked. But Delilah shook her head.

"I'm sorry," Delilah said finally. Her words came out in an uncertain croak.

"Okay," Sally replied. "Why are you sorry?"

"I'm sorry to be such a…freaking…mess." Delilah's words were broken with half-sobbed hiccups now, evidence of a complete and total meltdown.

Sally patted her hand. "We have plenty of time," she said. "I'm here. I'm not going anywhere."

Delilah wept on. Finally, she blew her nose and wiped her face. "Look." She raised her left hand in front of Sally. "Look at me!"

Sally looked. Delilah's hand was visibly shaking.

"What is that?" she asked, but Delilah only shook her head.

"I don't know what the hell it is!" she said. "All I know is that my career is over." Delilah looked at Sally balefully. "I just had to walk out in the middle of a job. I can't do fill. I can't do lines. I can't do any of it. I can't work, Sally."

The gravity of her words hung in the air between the two women. "Oh, man," Sally exhaled. "That is…wow, I'm so sorry."

Delilah closed her eyes. "And I don't have health insurance."

Sally nodded. Neither did she. "I'm so sorry."

Again, there was silence. "What's Tenika think?" Sally asked, filling the silence.

Delilah gave a snort. "She doesn't know. We're barely talking if you hadn't noticed."

The two women looked at each other. "You've got to tell her," Sally said softly.

Delilah studied her skirt and wiped at her face once more with the mangled tissue in her hands. She gave a heavy sigh. "Maybe."

"No maybe," Sally said. "You have to tell her. She's your partner."

Delilah looked directly at her. "Is she?"

Sally's hands fell into her lap with dismay. "Oh, my dear Delilah. This is not the time for righteous anger. You don't want to go through this alone. At least, that's how it looks from here."

Delilah gazed miserably at her hands once more. She'd resembled a lost little girl, sitting there slumped in her chair. "You need each other," Sally reminded her. "You know you do. Especially now."

There was dead silence in the kitchen, save for the ticking of the clock on the wall. "I don't know," Delilah finally said miserably. She stood up and folded her arms. "Okay, so suppose I tell her. She's *really* going to leave me then. Tenika already doesn't want to marry me, you know."

Sally looked at her friend sympathetically. "Things can change, honey."

Delilah's eyes flashed around the room as she continued. "I doubt it! I mean…look at me! I'm seriously damaged goods. I could have MS, or a brain tumor, or Parkinson's. I could have any number of things."

Delilah sat down, defeated once more. "It's all over," she declared. "All of it."

Sally cleared her throat. "Delilah, I've known you a very long time, right?"

Delilah nodded, still marinating in her misery.

"And we've been through a lot. Like at least six of my relationships, right?"

"Seven, I think."

"Yeah. Whatever," Sally continued, hitting her stride. "And when there was a real problem, never—*never*—did you tell me to go off by myself and lick my wounds. You always told me to go right back to my girlfriend and talk it through. Remember?"

Delilah sighed. *Yeah*, she remembered. She was not in the mood for tough love right now. It was hard enough just admitting to someone else that the problem was real. Tears began sliding down her face once more.

Sensing she may have come on too strong, Sally leaned forward and took her friend's hand. She gave it a squeeze. "What do you need right now?" she asked.

"I need to not have this fucking thing."

"Okay. What else?"

Delilah looked at her friend honestly doing the best she could for her, and she was moved. "Thank you," she said. "I guess…I guess I need to get a doctor's appointment. Probably get some tests, or whatever."

Sally nodded. "Alright. Anything else?"

Delilah hesitated. She knew Sally was right. Talking to Tenika would make this all so much more bearable, even if it was fraught with risk. Anyway, sooner or later Tenika would probably figure it out.

"I guess I need to talk to T," she admitted.

Sally nodded. "Okay. When you're ready. Just don't forget that you are not alone, Delilah. We've got your back. Both of us."

Delilah reached for her friend then, and the two women hugged. Delilah wiped her face with the back of her hand. "Do you think Tenika still loves me?"

Sally smiled. "I know she does," she said. "Without a doubt." She hesitated for a moment, uncertain whether she should say anything more.

"Trust her," she said finally. "And most of all, just trust yourself. Whatever this is, you already know how to get through it."

Delilah hugged her again. Then she blew her nose. "Thank you," she said.

And she really meant it.

Chapter Six

Well, that was depressing.
 With a sigh, Frankie closed the dating app she'd been looking at. Then she swiped it into oblivion for the rest of the day. Setting her jaw, she walked back to her spot at work. Today she was discretely policing a tech sales conference though, frankly, she found it hard to believe it merited undercover SFPD presence.

But this was San Francisco, a place where pretty much anything was possible. For reasons Frankie would never know, undercover policing was necessary.

She took a seat in the audience and looked around. Her bulletproof body armor was hot and itchy under her button-down shirt, and she was tired. Folding her arms across her chest, she studied the crowd, looking for anything out of place.

I might as well just give up on online dating, she thought as she sat there. It clearly wasn't going anywhere.

Frankie studied the perimeters of the room. For nearly three weeks now, there had been exactly no good prospects on the two apps she'd installed on her phone. Furthermore, for security reasons, she couldn't say much online about who she was, what she did, or even where she lived.

Her entire ad was an exercise in vagueness, including her picture. The picture showed her at the edge of a Sierra vista. She's out of focus, hiding in a dark hoodie.

Frankie had arrived in Oakland hopeful. After all, this was the East Bay, home to the biggest concentration of lesbians in the U.S., or possibly the world. There had to be somebody for her here somewhere. Hence her quick agreement to go out with Tasha the following night. It had been a pleasant surprise that Tasha had called.

Still something about Tasha didn't quite add up—all that business about working in a coffee bar. Frankie had seen enough at this point that nothing surprised her anymore. So maybe Tasha really was a barista, but Frankie seriously doubted it. This left the larger question. What did this woman actually do for a living?

Frankie slunk a little further down in her seat and attempted to look interested in the new AI financial planners being featured on the stage. Meanwhile, she continued to scope out the room in her peripheral vision, which was just a sea of tech geeks as far as the eye could see.

I have to stay positive, Frankie told herself because giving up or getting an attitude was simply not an option. But who knew? Maybe she really would find her girl at a garage. It was as good a place as any.

Until she did, Frankie was taking any help she could get.

*

Kate glanced at her phone. Then she looked again, disbelieving what she was seeing.

Stunned, Kate re-read the text. Then she read it again. And then a fourth time.

> *Your application for rental of our studio at 1341 Vermont Street, Oakland, has been accepted. Please call us to arrange a time to sign contracts, and provide checks for first and last months' rent. We look forward to having you.*

This wasn't supposed to happen.

Not at all. Kate wasn't supposed to actually *find* a place to live in the impossibly tight East Bay rental market. She was just going to go through the motions and pursue getting a place of her own so she could create a little more psychic space with Lizzy. By the time she'd searched for several months and found nothing, well...*then* it might actually be time to "move in" with Lizzy. Even though she already lived there.

Then she could finally relax about the whole U-Haul thing.

But now Kate suddenly found herself at a complicated cross-roads. Instantly, she was flooded with resistance. She no more wanted to move out of Lizzy's than fly to the moon. And yet... perhaps she really did need to. She kept telling herself, and Lizzy, that she did. This was where things got tricky.

Sitting there, Kate reviewed her options. She could take the room in the new apartment and honestly give herself some actual space in the relationship. Yet if she did so, she could risk losing Lizzy altogether, for Lizzy, of course, was not wild about this plan. Or she could let the rental go and commit more fully to Lizzy, in spite of the fact that she'd moved in much too soon. One way or another, she needed space.

Kate lifted her head and looked around the garage. Lizzy was deep under a hood on the other side of the garage, and Tenika was nowhere to be seen. She studied her girlfriend's long lean back as she bent over the Prius engine, tinkering in her navy coveralls. Kate sighed.

She didn't want to lose Lizzy—not at all. Life with Lizzy was exactly what she'd envisioned when she'd landed in the Bay Area eight years earlier. Lizzy was fun, kind, dependable, romantic, and unspeakably sexy. Their life together was rich and interesting.

She loved how they worked along beside each other at the garage. And how much they laughed. And the simple joy of finally being in the lesbian relationship she'd been wanting for all these years.

Anyway, Lizzy was her champion, perhaps the first true supporter she'd ever had.

The fact that Lizzy loved her ardently was something Kate was still getting used to. No, she loved Lizzy in return. She did. Even if she still felt this inexplicable pull in the other direction and living somewhere else. It was probably just her old primal fear kicking in.

Unless it wasn't.

The damnable thing was that she wasn't sure. Kate had never been great at putting her own needs before everyone else's. Not after being raised by two busy, half-besotted parents who had scant time for little Katy as they toddled off to the pub every afternoon. These were the moments when Kate felt massively confused.

Worse, now she was going to have to tell Lizzy about the text she'd just received. A wave of despair moved through Kate as she considered all the ramifications of her decision. If she didn't handle this correctly, Lizzy would break up with her for sure. Then would come the terrible day when she'd have to pack her bags and actually move out.

Inevitably, they would drift apart, victims of the distance between them. All of it would be heartbreakingly sad.

Yet, if Kate didn't move out and get the necessary distance from Lizzy to actually choose, once again, to live with her when the time was right, their nascent romance might die of its own accord.

She had only two weeks to make a decision and complete her move.

Kate glanced at the open text in her phone one more time. How had she gotten herself into this mess? Looking at Lizzy once more, she turned off her phone and put it away in her bag. Timing would be everything.

But first, she needed to decide if she would, in fact, be moving.

*

"Hey, sis," Tenika kissed Regina's cheek. Tenika saved up her visits with her ex-lover for times that were nothing less than emergencies.

"Glad to see you," Regina said, giving her a hug as they swung into their accustomed rhythm walking around Lake Merritt. Regina took a second look at her friend. "So what's up, T? You look like warmed over cat shit."

Tenika looked sideways at her. Regina made a face. "Just calling it like I see it."

"Yeah, well, don't. I'm all fucked up."

"I see that," Regina said, her voice softening. "Tell me what's up, baby girl."

Tenika sighed. "Things have gone from perfectly happy with Delilah to a shit storm in hell."

Regina sighed sympathetically. "Okay...what happened?"

"It's what didn't happen. I made it clear I was never going to marry her. And now basically...what day is it...Tuesday? She hasn't talked to me since Saturday morning. In fact, I've barely seen her. She just keeps disappearing all the time."

Regina studied her ex. Then she took the practical approach. "You guys still sleeping in the same bed?"

"Yeah," sighed Tenika. "But who knows for how long? I keep expecting to come home from work and find her packed up and moved out."

"Jesus."

"I know!" Tenika's voice cranked up in alarm. "This is serious."

"You tried flowers?"

"Red tulips—her favorite. She wouldn't even put them in a vase."

Regina shook her head. "Damn."

"Right? This whole thing has gotten hella crazy. I mean, she knew my deal when we got together. I made it as clear as day."

"Doesn't stop a girl from hoping," Regina pointed out. "I remember it well. And that was *before* marriage was legal."

"So what am I supposed to do?"

"Get over yourself, T. It's that simple. You want to spend your life with this girl?"

"Well," Tenika paused. "I mean, I thought I did. But when you put it that way." She wavered as she walked. Then she stopped and put her hands on her hips and looked at her friend. "You think I'm crazy not to marry her?"

Regina just kept on looking straight ahead as she walked on. "Completely." Now she glanced at Tenika. "This girl is the one, T. I told you once, and I'm going to say it again. She's got you dialed in."

"Okay," Tenika sighed heavily as she walked. "So tell me again how great marriage is."

Regina looked at her and laughed. "You seriously asking me?"

"I am." Tenika's voice had suddenly become smaller.

"Okay, then," said Regina, rising to the task. "Well, B.D. and I have been together for seven years, right? And there's no seven-year-itch, T. I can tell you that much."

"Seriously?"

"Yeah. It's a great relationship. We're happy. I mean, okay, you have your ups and downs in marriage, but you get through them." Regina glowed contentedly as she walked on, her voice rising. "Here's why you should get married, T. The minute you make that commitment, the petty shit just doesn't matter anymore. You just pull together and you deal with life…you know?" She looked at her ex. "When you get married, it's like you instantly grow up."

Tenika looked over at her. "Really?"

Regina nodded. "Really. You could use it," she added with a laugh.

"Okay! Okay!" Tenika waved away her friend's joke, like she was swatting at a fly. But she was also listening intently. If anyone knew how to make something like this work, it was Regina. "So, now what do I do?"

"I think it's what you don't do. Like don't panic. Don't go rushing in there with more flowers, or chocolates, or some damn craziness."

"And?"

"Well, think it through. First, decide if you'd marry her if you weren't so hell set against marriage in the first place."

"Well, Jesus, how do I figure that out?"

"You're the genius who made up the rule."

"Okay. Fair enough. I mean…" Tenika stopped and looked out at a pair of cormorants wading in the lake in front of them. Then she sighed heavily. "I just don't know. If I was all pro-marriage and everything…" Tenika's words trailed off. "Well, I honestly don't know what the hell I'd do," she finally admitted.

"You two talked this whole thing through yet?"

Tenika shook her head.

"Well, that's the first thing you've got to do," Regina asserted.

"I know," Tenika said with a nod. "I've got to wait up for her tonight, no matter how late she is."

Regina nodded her approval. "That's what I'm talking about, right there," she said. "Flowers and shit aren't going to solve this, T. You two just have to talk, talk, talk. Just talk *a lot*," she reasoned. "Then maybe at the end of it, you'll have something. Or you won't. But at least you're going to know exactly where you stand."

"Yeah, okay." Tenika looked out at the sun setting over the Oakland skyline. Then she looked back at her ex. "Thank you," she said.

"I got your back, sis."

"I know you do."

For a long moment, the two women hugged. Then once again, they began to walk.

*

Frankie studied the menu for several minutes. Then she glanced at her watch. Tasha was ten minutes late. A waitress came by for a drink order, and Frankie ordered a glass of cabernet sauvignon.

She craned her neck to look up the street through the enormous glass window in the front of Penrose. Tasha had wanted to meet here—a higher priced restaurant with an excellent menu. Normally Frankie wouldn't go to such a place on a first date, but this was the new Frankie she had on display.

Open. Fun. Up for anything. PTSD be damned.

At exactly twenty-two minutes past the hour, Tasha finally appeared. Frankie was now two-thirds of the way through her glass of wine. And that was a good thing because she was also well into a slow simmering case of anger. If there was anything that bothered her, it was people who were late. Especially on dates. And most especially in places with fourteen dollar glasses of wine.

Frankie cautioned herself to get a grip as she stood up and gave Tasha a quick hug.

"The drive over from Berkeley was ridiculous," she said, sitting down a little breathlessly. "Then the parking here in Grand Lake. Anyway, I should have taken surface. I'm totally sorry."

There…see? It was an innocent mistake. It was just traffic, Frankie told herself. "Don't worry about it," she said.

"Would you like a drink?" Frankie asked, offering the menu to Tasha. Tasha chose a glass of sparkling water with lemon.

Frankie pressed her now sweating palms into the linen napkin in her lap. "Nice place," she said, glancing around. "This menu is incredible. Everything comes from local farms."

"I come here fairly often. The flat iron is amazing."

There—that proved it. What barista could eat at Penrose? Frequently, no less?

Frankie glanced at her date still poring over the menu. Maybe she was independently wealthy, and she was into crafting lattes.

Tasha's sparkling water arrived, and Tasha inspected the glass. "Actually, could I have lime instead?" she asked with a smile. Then she shook her head as the waiter walked away. "There's no excuse for a crappy slice of lemon," she said in a low voice. "I mean, come on. This is California."

"At least it's sustainable," Frankie joked. Tasha did not laugh. Instead, she returned to her menu.

Dinner conversation progressed in fits and starts. By the end of the appetizers, Frankie had learned little about her date. Instead, she'd found herself rambling about fly fishing when she was a kid, her favorite pie (olallieberry), and why she'd register as an Independent in the next election. For the most part, Tasha had listened, her blue eyes fastened on Frankie as she spoke.

Frankie had gotten exactly nowhere in learning more about this woman. As their steaks arrived, she decided to take the bull by the horns. "So, Tasha," she said. "What do you do? I mean...what do you *really* do? For a living?"

The question hung out between them for a few moments. "What do you mean?" Tasha finally asked.

"Look, I know you're not a barista. What are you?"

Tasha shifted in her seat uncomfortably. Then she looked at Frankie. "Yeah, I'm not a barista. That's true." She looked at Frankie. "How did you know?"

Frankie folded her arms across her chest. "I just knew."

Tasha hesitated. "So have you got any pets?" she asked finally. "Pets? No."

Tasha visibly relaxed. Then she lowered her fork and looked around. "I'm a vet," she said in a low voice. "I'm sorry to lie. I don't generally reveal that on a first date. The minute people find out, they spend the rest of dinner talking about their cat's peeing habits and their dog's teeth."

"Wow." Now Frankie thought about the fact that she hadn't been particularly forthcoming with Tasha either. "I get it," she said.

Tasha looked more closely at Frankie, her blue eyes flashing. "So what about you, Frankie? What do you do? I don't think you've actually told me."

Frankie cut busily into her steak, avoiding her date's inquiring gaze. She should just tell Tasha. She seemed innocent enough. After all, this was the new Frankie. Trusting and open and all that. Right?

Frankie cleared her throat and looked at her date. "I'm a police officer," she said. "A sergeant with the SFPD."

Tasha visibly blanched. She put down her fork. Then she hesitated before she spoke. "Is this a joke or did someone set you up?"

"No—what?" Frankie was confused. The usual reaction was either curiosity or a request to see her weapon. But Tasha was visibly upset, and now Frankie wondered if she'd been wrong about her innocence.

"What is it?" Frankie repeated a little more urgently.

Tasha gave Frankie a dark look. "Have you ever heard of Police Scanner?"

Frankie swallowed and looked at Tasha. "Of course." Police Scanner was a royal pain in the butt of every officer on the squad. Mainly because they had to tiptoe around them all the time.

Police Scanner was a community activist organization entirely focused on every waking move of the Oakland Police Department. The minute anyone got shot, Police Scanner was on it like a pack of hungry hounds. They were always the first to report any injustices, large or small.

Tasha sat up a little more rigidly. She was not smiling. "I started it," she said.

"*You?*" Somehow, Frankie had always imagined some black mask wearing Antifa student from Berkeley was behind all the Police Scanner business.

"What, I'm not macho-looking enough? Jesus! As if it wasn't bad enough," Tasha muttered as she stood up and reached for her purse. "You're all the same, aren't you? Even the lesbians."

"Wait!" Frankie rose. "Just talk to me. You'll find out I'm not so bad. I mean…"

Tasha leveled her gaze at Frankie. "Have you killed anyone?"

Shit. How did they get here so fast?

Frankie sighed. Then she nodded in the affirmative. "I had to," she admitted.

"So they say," spat Tasha. "Don't even tell me what race your victim was."

Angrily, she put a few twenties on the table and drained her glass of sparkling water. Then looking at Frankie, she shook her head. "Too bad," she said. "However briefly, I thought you were hot."

With that, Tasha turned on her heel and stalked out, leaving a world-weary Frankie just sitting there.

There goes another one, she thought grimly.

She felt old indeed.

Chapter Seven

M indy Rose didn't have enough to do at night. That was the real problem. Padding around her darkened house in her bare feet, she felt yet another wave of loneliness wash through her. She badly needed some friends.

Yet, here was the dilemma. Where did you get friends when you were a controversial A-list lesbian and a TV personality at that? This was the sad fact of the matter. It was hard to trust people in her world because basically, they all wanted something. That's why having a live-in personal assistant had seemed like such a good idea at the time. Kate had been her helper, her fixer, and her friend all rolled into one.

Her new assistant, Cameron, seemed reasonable enough, but at moments like this, he was of little help. Once 6:00 PM rolled around every night, he was gone. Presumably off to cruise Grindr or whatever young gay men did with their free time these days. When he walked out the door of the garage each night, he never looked back.

Anyway, Mindy had learned her lesson. Employees—even long-standing ones—were not your friends. She'd made that mistake with Kate, and she'd be damned if she would ever do it again.

Yawning, Mindy sat down at her laptop and turned it on.
Kate.

Idly, Mindy Rose wondered if she'd been busted by ICE yet. It had been a good 48 hours since she'd filed the online report turning her in. Mindy knew it went through. There had been an automated message thanking her for her tip.

She opened Facebook and typed in Lizzy's name. Immediately, her profile page popped up. "Co-owner, Driven Garage," it said. She clicked on Lizzy's name. Kate's face swam into view. There they were together, posing by the lake, buying plums at the farmer's market, even walking in the redwoods.

"Goddammit," Mindy muttered. Where were the pleas for help on Lizzy's page, or even the requests for a good immigration lawyer? Didn't these two idiots realize what kind of danger they were both in? Mindy was quite sure Lizzy was employing Kate under the table. She had to be, even if there were no pictures of Kate at the garage posted online.

Apparently, everything was still just ducky in Happy Valley.

Mindy shut her laptop with disgust and went off to look for ice cream.

There had to be some around here somewhere.

*

Tenika folded her arms and suppressed a yawn. She looked at the clock on the mantel. It was close to eleven. She'd been sitting and dutifully waiting for Delilah for the last two hours.

Tenika had no idea where she was, but tonight she was going to talk to her, no matter what.

Moving over to a hard chair at the dining room table, she sat down again. She would stay awake, no matter what it took.

She'd long ago turned off the television. Instead, Tenika preferred the comfort of silence. There was a lot to think about as she sat there.

Why, for instance, didn't she want to marry Delilah? Was this just some old tape she was still carrying around from her early twenties when she made up all her supposed rules about life?

Now, years later, the rule had an out-of-date feel. Still, Tenika remained cautious. There was a lot at stake to simply erase a rule that, so far at least, had served her well.

She thought about the fact that Regina had once wanted to marry her, long before the Supreme Court ruling on marriage equality. Then it was February of 2004, and marriage was something you could do, however briefly, because the mayor of San Francisco had suddenly made it possible.

In her giddiness to rush to the altar, Regina had overlooked a simple fact: she and Tenika weren't actually that compatible. But her mother and Tenika's auntie adored each other. And the big family barbecues out in Concord were actually a lot of fun. That's when they forgot about inconvenient things, like their lack of sexual compatibility and Regina's need to control.

That time, Tenika's personal ban on marriage had been a godsend, and very necessary. Especially because all around them, lesbians and gays were racing to San Francisco City Hall to do the deed before that particular door slammed shut. And now, many years later, a lot of those couples were no longer together.

Marriage is for life, she reminded herself. Even now. The fact that she didn't want to marry Delilah by no means meant she didn't want to spend her life with her. She did. Or so she thought.

Still, forever really was a very long time.

Tenika looked up as a key turned in the door. A moment later, Delilah walked in. She put her messenger bag down on the floor and gazed at Tenika. "Hi," she said softly.

Then, surprisingly, she didn't bolt for the bedroom as Tenika feared she might. Instead, she sat down on the couch. "Are you okay?" Tenika asked.

Delilah looked at the floor for a moment as one tear, then two, began to slide down her face. "Honey?" asked Tenika leaning forward. Silent sobs shook Delilah's body, and in an instant,

Tenika was sitting beside her. She put her arm around her lover and held her close.

Delilah did not resist. Instead, she melted into her shoulder and cried a little harder. "I'm so sorry," Tenika said, pulling her closer. "I never wanted to hurt you, baby."

"I know," Delilah managed to say. Pulling back, she pulled out a handkerchief and wiped her face. She hiccuped slightly and blew her nose. "That's not why I'm crying. I mean, I'm sad about that and pretty pissed, too, but…"

Tenika pushed a few stray strands of Delilah's hair off her face and looked at her with concern. "But what?"

Delilah just shook her head, unable to speak. Tenika sighed and held her a little closer. "Okay," she said.

They went on this way for some time. At one point, Sally looked in from the kitchen, and then retreated to her book at the kitchen table. *God bless her*, Tenika thought to herself. For if there was one thing she knew, there was no hurrying Delilah. When she was ready, she would speak, and not a moment sooner.

As she sat there holding Delilah, Tenika had time to reflect. She thought about all they had been through in the last seven years. She thought about how reasonable it was for Delilah to want to get married.

After all, they knew that certain thing that all committed couples realized sooner or later. They belonged together, no matter what. They were connected, woven together through some kind of crazy eternal bond that had sewn their souls together. There was no getting around it.

This was, indeed, real.

Finally, Delilah raised her head to speak. She gave a shuddering breath, then she leaned back against her chair and looked straight ahead. "There's something wrong with me," she said.

A zing of frightened electricity shot through Tenika's body and she sat up. "What are you talking about?"

Delilah sighed. Then she held up her left hand. "Look."

Immediately, Tenika reached for it, but Delilah pushed her away. "No," she said. "*Look* at my hand."

It was trembling hard. In fact, it was outright shaking.

"What the fuck?" Tenika said, studying her hand. "What is that?"

"I don't know, but it started last weekend," Delilah said. Then she paused. "After we talked."

"Whoa," Tenika exhaled. "You got a doctor's appointment yet?"

Delilah shook her head, and Tenika was not surprised. In Delilah's world, doctors were usually low on the list after naturopaths, crystal healers, and shamans. "Honey, this could be serious. You've got to get to a doctor."

"I know!" Delilah snapped irritably. "And who has health insurance? Not me! I can't even find a doctor who will see me."

Tenika crossed her arms. "Oh, come on! They have to see you. That's ridiculous."

"Fine," said Delilah, her voice rising testily. "I've called eight of them. You go find some doctor who will see me."

"Happy to." Tenika stood and began to pace. Then suddenly, she sat down beside her lover again. "Why didn't you tell me?"

Delilah gave a sarcastic laugh. "Oh, I was supposed to rush to you after the big 'I will not marry you' pronouncement? T, seriously. I mean, what if I have something major like Parkinson's or MS or…whatever. Then you're really going to be done with me."

"Baby girl, come on," said Tenika, taking her hands. "I love you, and I am far from done here. Just because I don't want to get married doesn't mean I want to leave. Not at all! I keep trying to explain that to you."

"And I keep trying to say I don't get it. I mean…I'm fucked up here." Delilah's voice rose in utter frustration. "I need a partner to get me through this. A committed partner."

"I *am* a committed partner," Tenika insisted. "Hell, I'm a lot more committed to you than any other woman I've been with."

That stopped Delilah. She looked at Tenika intently. "Really?"

"Really."

Tenika reached for her hand, and Delilah took it. Then leaning forward they kissed. Lips meeting, tongues touching, love pouring forth once again. "Come on, baby," Tenika said, pulling her lover close. "We're going to get through this. Maybe it's nothing."

"Glad you think so," Delilah sighed. Then she looked at her partner. "I've been so scared," she admitted, her voice shaking.

"I'm here. And I'm telling you, I am not leaving."

"You sure?"

"Of course I'm sure." Tenika ran her hand through Delilah's hair tenderly. "Not only am I sure, I'm personally going to find out what this fucking thing is, and we're going to deal with it."

"Really?"

"Of course. We're going to start by finding a doctor. And not just any doctor—we're going to get the right one."

"I saw my chiropractor, and she adjusted me."

"And?"

Delilah looked down. "Nothing. T, what if it's some disease? You know I could have been poisoned at work—from the disinfectant. Anyway, that's the other thing."

"What?"

Delilah looked down at her trembling hand in her lap. "Basically, I have to quit my job."

Tenika sat back slightly. "What? Are you sure?"

"T...I can't even draw a straight line, much less ink one. I have to tell Rhonda." Delilah began to cry softly once more. "I don't know if I'll ever get my chair back. What if it never stops shaking?"

"Whoa. Jesus, this is serious," Tenika rose once more and began to pace. "Okay...I'm really getting the whole picture now."

Delilah glanced up at her wearily. "Good. Because basically, I'm out of ideas."

Tenika nodded. "Trust me, honey. I got this."

Reaching out her hand once more, she took Delilah's. Then she pulled her up off the couch. "Come on," she said, pulling Delilah in close for a hug. Tenika wrapped her arms around her lover, burying her face in the warm contour of her neck. "I've got you, baby. We're going to do this together."

Delilah smiled once more before she kissed her love, and Tenika felt her entire body relax.

It was good to be back.

*

Kate leaned back in the steaming tub filled with Epsom salts and closed her eyes. Sinking down, she let the warm water loosen her shoulders and comfort her neck.

Gone for just a moment was the pressing question on the table. Should she move out…or should she stay?

Once again her mind leapt into its worn racetrack of possibilities. Wearily, Kate reviewed them again. Then she closed her eyes. She wanted to be done with this conversation. She just wanted certainty.

Anyway, what was she going to tell Lizzy? Lizzy still didn't know about the apartment she'd been offered. And at this exact moment in time, Kate was leaning towards taking it.

A move would be a clean break. It would permit some air to circulate in their relationship so they could both get their feet underneath them. And there was a new development that seemed to validate the move.

Suddenly, Kate had a new marketing client, as well.

The freelance offer from a small vineyard in Berkeley came about through nothing less than serendipity. She'd opened the emailed offer only a few hours earlier, and it was perfect. They asked no tricky immigration questions. They loved her connection to Mindy Rose. And they wanted to hire her for regular part-time work. She'd met them through a contact at a networking mixer two days earlier.

They were offering just enough to pay most of her monthly expenses, the balance of which her work for Driven would cover. And this certainly made it possible to attract additional clients.

Kate knew she would be just fine—as long as she said yes to all of it. If she wanted this, and it appeared she did, she would have to tell Lizzy tonight. Waiting would just complicate everything.

Kate thought hard for a moment. If she could create a romantic, intimate moment between them, Lizzy would understand. She wouldn't take it personally. She would see the possibilities, perhaps even the benefit of such a move. Who knew? Lizzy might even decide it was a good idea.

Kate picked up the sponge from the water and squeezed it over her face. Warm water cascaded across her cheeks, her nose, her forehead, her hair, easing her worries. There was apparently a light at the end of this long, uncertain tunnel.

Kate would say yes, and she *would* tell Lizzy tonight.

Somehow she would make it happen. She had to because her new life had just arrived.

*

Lizzy rolled onto her back and stared at the ceiling in the darkness. Beside her, Kate finally slept peacefully. She listened to the steady rhythm of her partner's breathing.

Lizzy sighed. Something was wrong. She could feel it. Kate had curled up beside her at bedtime, lying in her arms as usual. And yet, Kate was also strangely silent. She said she was exhausted, but then she shifted and twitched and rolled this way and that for a long time. There was no easy sleep for either of them.

When she'd finally asked Kate if she was all right, Kate had hesitated for just the slightest of moments before she answered yes. In that hesitation lay the truth, and Lizzy knew it.

Something was clearly amiss. But what was it?

Lizzy pondered the possibilities as she lay there. Kate was worried about her immigration situation, but that was an old worry. Why would this suddenly keep her up now? Kate was also worried about money, yet who wasn't short of cash in their circle? Lizzy had already assured her that she would help as she could, until Kate had regular income coming in again.

Still, she could feel Kate pulling away from her.

Lizzy had tried not to cling and grasp. She'd done everything she could to be the perfect girlfriend. She'd been accommodating, protective, fun, sexy. She'd even employed Kate in a time of need. And, of course, she'd loved her.

Lizzy rolled over and closed her eyes again. Maybe she was worrying too much. If Kate moved out, it wouldn't necessarily be the end. On the other hand, where was she going to go with few reserves and little hope of finding a place in the East Bay?

No, Kate would probably stay right here. At least Lizzy hoped she would. Then maybe she'd still have a chance. Still, one thing dogged her mind that she couldn't shake.

It was the vast chasm of silence that had followed each time she'd told Kate she loved her.

Rolling over again, Lizzy closed her eyes in an attempt to get back to sleep. God, she wanted this to work out. She really, truly, absolutely did.

Yet, all she could do was wait and see.

Chapter Eight

S ally threw down an armload of bed linens on the couch and began her nightly ritual once again.

Unfolding the bottom sheet, she gave it a shake and tucked it around the cushions on the couch. Much as she was grateful for this soft couch to land on, this routine was getting old. Still, when you have nothing, you don't get to really have an opinion. Smiling, Sally thought of her minister, Revelo, and his affirmation for the last service she'd attended at the Heart and Soul Center of Light.

I've got nothing to complain about.

She actually didn't, she reminded herself. Okay, so…yes… her bank account had now officially slid to three figures, but she'd been here many times before. And, yes, plans did need to be made immediately to make more money. But right now, right here, Sally was fine. And wasn't that all that mattered?

She had food in the refrigerator. She had dear friends helping her get back on her feet. And she had her God-given skills which were, well, eclectic. There was the dog walking. That had been good for a while until a particularly anxious Jack Russell terrier bit her in the calf. And there was the Reiki, which had its adherents. The only issue was that she constantly had to drum up new clients wherever she went. Marketing had never been Sally's strong suit.

Through all of it, Sally never lost faith, whether she worked as a nanny, or a waitress, or she stood on the street with a clipboard, canvassing for the cause of the minute. Quite the opposite, Sally always felt like she was doing the right thing. For in each moment, it actually *was* the right thing.

In other words, there was no long game here. There was only now. Hence the tattoo Delilah had given her a few years back.

Nunc Vitae. Life is now.

Sally now walked to the coat closet in the front hall and pulled her pillow from the top shelf. At least Tenika and Delilah appeared to have worked through their stuff. She could hear them in the bedroom. Their low voices were punctuated by long silences and the occasional laughter. As she'd thought, talking was all it took. With a smile, she thought about something Tenika had said.

You should be a life coach. It was so like her friend to be thinking ahead. To try to fix her future as best she could. She wasn't a life coach, of course, nor would she become one.

Sally was a psychic, despite her efforts to hide from this truth. Still, it burned on in the back of her consciousness, year after year, like a small persistent flame that never, ever went out. The psychic work was just so intensely intimate and so very vulnerable. She had a hard time imagining doing it for anyone besides her closest friends. And yet, there it was, always rattling around in her head.

Being a medium was Sally's true work. She figured she'd get to it when she was ready and not one moment sooner. This was how it was with guided work—you had to just surrender. And then finally, when the time was right, it flowed with ease and grace.

Fluffing out the down comforter across the couch, Sally pulled back the corner and made her small nest as inviting as possible. When you came right down to it, she liked living lean. There was a cleanness to not having a house, or a mortgage, or a pet, or even a credit card. It protected her from the harsh realities that more ambitious people suffered.

She'd been living out of a suitcase for several years now as she wandered here and there. Sally told herself that experiences and relationships were her furniture—her stuff. And most of the time, she believed it. When you lived this way, luxury was a long hot bath, or maybe a good book taken from a free book box on the street.

Still, Sally imagined there would come a day when she'd be forced to stop the travels and the adventures, and focus on the simple math of life. Then she would finally relinquish her backpack, with its pack towel, its well-worn water bottle, and the single wrinkle-free dress stuffed in the bottom.

Then she would listen closely to the rhythm of life, and she would say yes. That's when Sally would finally pull her last card out of her hat and begin her true work.

Heading off to brush her teeth, she yawned. Tomorrow would reveal itself, and with it would come the next few feet of the path ahead of her. For now, there was nothing to do but let go.

Sally smiled at the thought. That really was the point, wasn't it?

*

Tenika scrolled down the long list of possible causes of tremors. "I'm telling you, honey, I've been through them all repeatedly," Delilah said from the bed.

Tenika kept on scrolling. "I hear you. I just have to see this for myself."

Now she turned to her lover. "What's that stuff you use at work?"

"Madicide. I already looked it up."

"And?"

Delilah patted the bed beside her. "Right now what you can do for me is right here."

Tenika smiled. Standing up, she snapped the laptop shut. "Oh yeah?" she asked.

Delilah smiled. "Yeah. I need some love."

"Don't we all?" asked Tenika wearily, pulling off her tee shirt and her underwear. Climbing in to bed, she took her lover in her arms. Then she sighed as she looked at Delilah and felt her naked body nestle into her own. "I'm so freaking glad you're still speaking to me," she said.

Delilah shook her head. "What else can I do?" she asked. Then leaning over, she kissed Tenika. "I can't exactly stay mad. Anyway, what's the point?"

"You got that right." Tenika said. Pulling her close, she studied the ceiling. It felt so perfect to have Delilah in her arms again. It had been a desert while she'd been angry. "So what's the deal with the Madacide anyway?"

"Sneezing, headaches. Watery eyes. That's about it. Anyway, I always wear latex."

Tenika exhaled slowly. "Don't worry," she said, kissing Delilah's head. "We're gonna get it."

"I know we will." Delilah whispered. "I'm sorry."

"Me, too," said Tenika. "It was one long cold winter while you weren't talking to me, baby. I'll tell you that."

"I know," said Delilah. "We just belong together, you know?"

"I do know. And I'm glad you get it." Tenika looked into her lover's face once again and saw all the worry and the fear there. "Oh, baby, don't worry so much. I've got you."

"I know you do," Delilah whispered as she closed her eyes. "And I've got you."

Pulling her tight, Tenika made herself a small promise. She was going to fight for this woman, this love of hers. She was going to help Delilah get over this thing.

No matter what it took, she was going to do it.

*

Peering at her phone in the darkness, Frankie opened the online dating app. What else was there to do at 3:48 in the morning?

She'd woken half an hour earlier, heart pounding and yelling in her sleep. Again, there was the replay of that night at Ocean

Beach. Like clockwork it appeared, this nightmare, forcing her to relive every last moment of getting out of her patrol car and finding the body of the naked twelve-year-old. Her mutilated body, lying there in the sand. A hysterical woman who'd found the girl while walking her dog stood nearby, sobbing loudly.

Weirdly, the dream always happened in slow motion as Frankie climbed out of the car and slowly approached. Then she checked the body to make sure she was no longer breathing.

Then, each time, Frankie woke up. Inevitably, she lay there for the next hour and a half, wide awake and disturbed. But now she was heading for that quiet island of hope, her online dating inbox.

She badly needed a shot of confidence after the blind date from hell with Tasha. But lately her inbox had become a somewhat scary place, as well. The usually ripe possibility of finding new love had withered right up.

There had been the married straight woman looking for a polyamorous threesome, and the charming but suspect French woman who was pretty enough but sounded like a total borderline. Then there was someone named Dora who kept showing up and asking painfully awkward questions.

Other than that, there was…nothing. Just crickets. It had gotten to the point that Frankie didn't even want to browse the other profiles.

After the Tasha run-in, she had a new uncertainty, as well. Exactly when should she reveal that she was in law enforcement? It just didn't seem like there *was* any other good time beside the first date. Not when you considered how many crazies there were out there, cruising online and hating cops. These women deserved to know her deal sooner rather than later.

Anyway, Frankie certainly couldn't blow her cover and put the missing information in her profile. Still, when she waited to reveal this rather large fact about her life, resentment always followed. The women she was interested in didn't like being surprised.

Somehow it was a major faux pas, like lying about your age.

When you got right down to it, there actually wasn't any good time to reveal her interesting profession. Frankie was damned if she didn't, and damned if she did. That's just the way it was.

At least some women went for the uniform.

Tentatively, she clicked on the inbox and examined the contents. Yet another message from Dora suggested they meet. *No, no, and no,* Frankie thought to herself. With a swipe, she removed Dora's access to her page.

Then she put her phone down with a sigh. This online dating thing was going nowhere. If she wanted to meet someone, it was going to have to be live. She'd have to go where the lesbians went. And where would that be, given that the Bay Area's last lesbian bar, the Lex, closed in 2016?

Frankie had no idea, other than the occasional dance or Ladies Night at one of the men's bars.

No, these were hard times for sure in the lesbian monoculture. This was when she missed her late wife more than ever. Pulling a pillow close, Frankie rolled over and attempted to quiet her racing mind. She would find someone. She would. She had to. Anyway, worrying now would do nothing more than exhaust her.

Love would help put her back together. With the right woman, maybe her nightmares would even end.

Even if hope was basically futile, it was really all she had.

Chapter Nine

Mindy closed the door to her office and waited, phone in hand, while government Muzak filled her ear. She hated being put on hold.

First, she began to tap her foot. Then, finally, she gave up and began to pace.

What the hell was taking so long?

A voice finally crackled onto the line. "Ma'am?" asked the sterile sounding woman.

"Just tell me. Have you done anything or not?" Mindy pressed.

"Actually, ma'am..."

"Just answer the question," Mindy interrupted. "I emailed in this tip nearly 72 hours ago. Are you people even reading your inbox?"

There was a pause at the other end. "We have no record of your submission," the official voice said.

"Oh, come on!" Mindy exploded. "Seriously? Jesus! What's it take? I *know* this woman is being paid illegally. Just take my information right now. This is a very serious federal offense. The illegal I'm talking about is named Kate Morahan."

"I'm sorry, ma'am. Due to the volume of tips we are processing...," the voice droned.

"Hey, do you even realize who I am?" Mindy interrupted. "This is Mindy Rose, the internationally known race car driver and two-time Indy winner, and I'm..."

"Please submit your tip at www dot...," the voice on the other end of the line intoned.

But Mindy didn't stick around for the rest of the rote response. Instead, she hung up.

"Screw you," she snarled at her phone. Then she slumped in her chair, momentarily defeated. What she really needed now was someone else to take this horror show and run with it. Specifically, she needed an immigration lawyer, and a highly aggressive one at that.

Reaching for her phone, Mindy opened her browser and once again began to surf.

The matter of Kate's immigration status was far from over.

*

"Frankie!" Kate's voice rang out encouragingly as Frankie peered into the shadows of Driven. It appeared both the owners were out.

"Lunchtime," explained Kate. "But perhaps I can help."

"Ah, right." Frankie stuck her hands in her pockets and glanced around. "Just need a new pair of wiper blades," she explained. Truthfully, she'd been looking for any excuse to get back to the now much-appreciated customer conversation corner. That very perfect place where she'd met Tasha not too long ago had been on her mind.

As if on cue, Kate asked, "Did you and Tasha happen to connect?"

Frankie blanched slightly. *Jesus—did these people know her every move?* "Oh, well...yeah, I did meet her here, didn't I?" she murmured. But Kate brushed off her reply.

"Tasha is a very dynamic woman, to be sure," she noted. "Did she tell you she's a veterinarian? And such pretty eyes. At any rate, how are you doing?" Kate asked, smoothly segueing. She flashed Frankie a broad, beaming smile. "Presumably you brought your car in as well?"

"I did." Frankie seized on something tangible to talk about with gusto. "Yeah, I don't know if you guys do parts? Like windshield wiper blades?"

"Certainly," Kate said with a smile.

"We do everything. But by 'we' I don't mean me, personally. I don't get involved with the cars, you know. But Lizzy and Tenika should be back momentarily. Come have a sit. I'll make us a cup of tea."

Frankie's whole nervous system relaxed at the invitation. Of course, she'd like a cup of tea. In fact, she'd love one. And a girlfriend, while she was at it.

Kate inspected the basket of tea bags. "All I have is black tea at the moment, I'm afraid. Would that suit you?"

"Me? Oh yeah, sure. The more caffeine the better," she joked. Frankie sat down a little awkwardly on the love seat. For a moment, there was silence between them.

Soon the kettle was heating, and Kate had joined her. "So how goes it, Frankie?" she asked, settling cozily into a nearby armchair. "I'm glad to see you're back with us."

"Oh, you know. Life in Oakland. It's good." Frankie rubbed her hands together and cleared her throat a bit self-consciously. "This is nice," she said, glancing around.

Kate raised her eyebrows inquiringly. "This?"

"The conversation corner," Frankie said, noting the sign on the wall. "Great idea."

Kate smiled. "Sounds like you and Tasha did get together."

"Wasn't a fit," Frankie said tersely.

"That's fine," Kate said easily. "Plenty more fish in the sea, as they say."

There was a pause. Then Frankie heard some improbable words spill out of her mouth. "I'd love to find one of them," she said. *Where in God's name did that come from?*

"Lovely," Kate said. "Then you'll have to keep coming back,

won't you? And we'll be delighted to see you anytime, Frankie. Just come by. Even without your car. Some very nice women gather here these days…just to do the puzzles and chat. It's lovely."

Lizzy's voice rang out from the doorway just then. "Hey Frankie!"

Within a moment, Lizzy had disappeared in the back, checking for the right length wiper blade. And within another moment, the needed blades were snapped into place and Frankie was shelling out fifteen dollars. Meanwhile, Frankie sipped tea and chatted amiably with Kate.

Kate now approached as Frankie waited for change. "Got an idea for you," she said. "Would you be open to a blind date, Frankie?"

Frankie glanced up sharply from her transaction. *Blind date?* An unaccustomed sense of rightness, and inevitability, washed over her.

What the hell was this?

"Honey…" Lizzy cautioned, but Kate waved her partner off. "I've got a woman in mind who might find you very interesting," she said. "Our friend Sally is single. A lovely woman. And *so* very interesting. She's got many, many gifts. Gifts I think you might be partial to," Kate added mysteriously.

Frankie shrugged. "What do I have to lose?" she asked rhetorically. Meanwhile, her mind was spinning a thousand revolutions a second.

A blind date? Seriously? Desperation was now kicking in.

Behind Frankie, Lizzy was now staring at Kate with widening eyes, but Kate carried on nonplussed. "Shall I ask her to come by the garage?" she asked. "Or perhaps you might meet for tea or a glass of wine if she's game?"

"Oh," Frankie said, drawing herself up. "Just…here…" She grabbed one of the business cards for the garage and scrawled her number on the back quickly. Then she handed it to Kate. "Have her call me."

Then, in a flash, Frankie hurried out of the garage, mission complete.

They heard the door click shut as Frankie left, and Lizzy looked at Kate, dumbfounded. "What on earth are you doing?"

"You know perfectly well!" she retorted. "I'm creating another customer for life."

"But...but what if they don't like each other?"

"Not our fault," Kate countered. "She's already met one 'not a fit' in the conversation corner. And sure enough, she's back. Even with a bit of business for us. The important thing is that we care, Lizzy. And that we deliver."

Lizzy exhaled sharply. "Okay," she said, shaking her head. "I just hope this is a good idea."

"Trust me, love," her partner said. "I haven't let you down yet, have I?"

"Nope," Lizzy reasoned. "Guess not." Then leaning over with a smile, she kissed Kate on the lips. "I love having you here," she said, and Kate smiled shyly up at her.

Then turning away, a wave of regret washed through Kate. She still hadn't told Lizzy about moving out. That would have to happen tonight.

Without fail.

But now, it was time to call Sally.

*

Delilah stood at the entrance of Rhonda's office and cleared her throat. She hated conversations like this. "Uh, Rhonda?" she asked. "Could I speak to you?"

Amidst the cozy clutter in her tiny office, her boss glanced over her shoulder. "Sure, come on in," she said. There was no place to sit so Delilah stepped one foot inside the door and just stood there. She clasped her hands behind her back to make her tremor less noticeable. She studied the inflatable brontosaurus suspended over Rhonda's head and her collection of bobble head dolls, mostly scored at Giants games, lined up on the windowsill.

Her silver-haired boss was an approachable woman. A large tattoo-covered dyke always seen in denim overalls, Rhonda was known for being strong and kind. She'd personally been inking people for decades, and she had brought up quite a few artists, Delilah among them.

Over the past four years, Rhonda had been more like a big sister or even a mother to her. In fact, there was nothing Delilah wouldn't do for her boss. Now, having to ask for leave from work was hard. Delilah knew exactly how much it would screw up the flow of customers coming into the studio.

Within a few days, there would be a back up, and before long, customers lost. It would all be Delilah's fault.

Rhonda looked at her encouragingly. "What's up, kiddo?" Then she turned and regarded Delilah more closely. "Something's wrong," she announced. Now Rhonda spun in her chair and turned in earnest towards Delilah. "What's going on?" she asked, at which Delilah promptly burst into tears.

"Uh...I don't know...exactly," Delilah said, hurriedly trying to push the tears off of her cheeks.

Don't cry, for God's sake! Delilah shook her head vehemently, trying to stop her tears. This was just making the whole thing worse.

"What on earth?" Rhonda asked. Standing now, she reached out and put her hand on Delilah's arm. "What is it, honey?"

Delilah inhaled miserably. She needed to fight the incredible twisting in her gut and her sense of imminent doom, and just tell her boss what was going on. She reminded herself that she was doing the right thing.

Still, all Delilah could do was stand there, frantically trying not to cry. "I'm sorry," she finally said.

Rhonda looked at her worriedly. "Would you please tell me what's going on? Do you need a raise or something?"

Delilah laughed in spite of herself. "No, Rhonda, I wish it was that simple." She took another breath. "I've got this weird thing." Reluctantly, she held her trembling hand up in front of Rhonda. "Look," she said.

"Jesus," muttered Rhonda. "You know what this is?"

Tears began to move down Delilah's cheeks in earnest. "No."

Her boss sighed heavily. "Oh, baby, come here," she said, opening her arms to Delilah for a hug.

Delilah moved into her embrace, and let her old friend and mentor comfort her. Rhonda pulled back and looked at her. "You tell Tenika what's going on?" she asked.

"Yeah, I told her. She's being amazing." Delilah took the red bandanna Rhonda pulled from her pocket, and she blew her nose. "Well, that's good," Rhonda said. "Shit—I wish I had a health insurance plan for you."

"I don't need insurance. Well, I mean I do. But what I really need is to not be inking people. I…I can't," she finally admitted.

"Of course," Rhonda said. "Take off as long as you need." She looked at Delilah with concern. "You really have no idea what it is?"

"No. I can't even find a doctor who will take me."

"Well, Rennie will know someone who will. That much we can do for you." Renata was Rhonda's partner, and a nurse at one of the big medical complexes on Pill Hill.

Delilah smiled. "That would be amazing," she said. This much she certainly hadn't expected. But, of course, Rhonda was just this sort of person.

There was a pause. "Will you take me back when I get this sorted out?" Delilah now asked in a small voice.

"Are you kidding? An artist like you? Of course, I will," Rhonda said. "Nobody can do the sunsets or the flowers like you,

Delilah." Rhonda paused and studied her for a moment. "You don't have disability, do you?"

Delilah shook her head. *What tattoo artist got disability insurance,* she wondered. "It's okay. I'll figure something out," she replied. But Rhonda didn't answer. Instead, she pulled a large business checkbook out of her desk and opened it.

Delilah watched as Rhonda filled out a check, then tore it from the book. Turning back to Delilah, she handed it to her. It was a check for a thousand dollars. Delilah looked at the check, disbelieving what was in her hand.

Overcome, Delilah attempted to hand the check back. "No. No wait, Rhonda. I can't possibly accept this."

"You certainly can, honey. It's for the first few months of insurance," Rhonda said. "Maybe you'll even get back here by then."

Rhonda closed Delilah's fingers around the check and pushed it back towards her more firmly. Then she looked into her mentee's eyes. "You've got a lot of inking ahead of you, baby. Take the money. You need it."

Tears sprang into Delilah's eyes, and she knew Rhonda was right. "Thank you," she whispered.

"You're going to be okay. I know it," insisted Rhonda.

Delilah took a shaky breath and smiled weakly. "Thank you," she repeated.

Maybe she really was going to be okay. For just one moment, Delilah allowed herself one tiny glimmer of hope.

Then hugging her boss, she sent up a small prayer of thanks. Perhaps she really would be okay.

*

Kate picked up a dish towel and the newly washed sauté pan beside the sink. Taking a breath, she began to dry it. "Sweetheart?"

Lizzy smiled from a sink full of suds. "Yeah?"

Kate breathed back the mountain of butterflies that had been building in her gut for the last two hours since they'd got home. The night had gone well so far. She'd made a lovely chicken stir fry, and steered the conversation this way and that into safe and comforting territory. But now it was time for the bombshell that she knew would derail everything.

Lizzy smiled at her. She pulled the chef's knife from the suds and giving it another swipe with the sponge, rinsed it off and placed it on the counter to dry. "What's on your mind?"

Kate hesitated for a nanosecond. *Just do it,* she commanded herself. "You remember that apartment I looked at?" she began.

Lizzy paused, her sudsy hands poised above the sink. "Yeah," she replied. Lizzy's expression went blank.

Kate looked at her. "Well…actually, I'm taking it," she announced. "I'm moving out next week."

The two women looked at each other. There was utter silence between them, and Lizzy's face was now awash with panic. Finally, she sighed and shook her head.

"Oh, Kate," was all she said. She appeared to be crestfallen.

"It's not you—and I don't want to break up! I really don't!" Kate insisted.

Lizzy looked unconvinced as she turned off the faucet. Putting her hands on her hips, she stared out the window in front of her. "But you don't want to stay, either."

"Sweetheart, please. I've explained it. I need a space of my own. I just need a way to get my feet on the ground." Kate paused, her heart racing. "I need to be able to come back to you on my own terms—to really choose this entire thing, if that makes sense. I need to have some free will, don't you see?"

Lizzy licked her lips distastefully. "All I see is we've got a good thing and you're rejecting it."

Kate took a step towards her lover and put her hands on her shoulders, but Lizzy brushed her off and crossed her arms defiantly.

"No! I'm not rejecting it," Kate insisted. "I'm trying to choose it, right?"

"Maybe," Lizzy sighed. "If I seriously squint, I can kind of sort of see it. But not really, Kate. Not at all."

Lizzy strode off towards the living room. "Don't wait up for me," Kate heard her say over her shoulder. Then she watched as Lizzy pulled her bike down from the hook and took her helmet and her jacket out of the closet. Within another moment, Lizzy was gone, seeking her therapy. A bike ride at night.

Miserably, Kate sunk into the couch, feeling as alone as she ever had. This was necessary.

It just was.

That was all she knew.

*

Delilah pulled up to the house on her bike and wove her way through the front gate. Tenika was already home.

Good.

That way she could confirm her lack of employment as soon as she walked in. Sometimes ripping off the Band-Aid was the only way to go.

Pulling her bike up to the door, Delilah paused as she fished out the house keys with her good hand. She was probably done with bike riding, too, now that she thought about it. On the way home, she noticed she'd begun to wobble.

Screw all of it, she thought with abandon. What she really wanted right now was sex, weed, and sweet relief.

"Honey?" she called as she pushed her bike inside. "You home?"

"Back here, baby!" Tenika's voice rose from the kitchen. The unmistakable aroma of oxtail stew filled her nose.

"Are you cooking?" she asked, coming into the kitchen.

"Figured you needed some decent home cooking," Tenika said. Then taking Delilah in her arms, she kissed her mouth.

Tenderly, Tenika looked into her face. "You okay?" she asked as she brushed away a stray strand of hair.

"No." Delilah shook her head. "Things are fucked," she said. She looked up at her partner. "I told Rhonda I have to stop working."

Tenika sighed. "Oh, baby. Are you sure?"

Delilah nodded. "I have to stop before I screw up the next job. I've already had two close calls. I can't get the lines straight." A sob caught in her throat. "I don't want to stop," she said. Two large tears now slid down her cheeks.

"Come here." Tenika folded her arms more tightly around Delilah. "It's okay," she soothed.

"Not okay, T—not okay! I don't know what the fuck I'm going to live on."

"I've got you," Tenika murmured into the top of her head, and Delilah looked up at her.

"This could go on for months, or…well, shit, who knows? Maybe forever." Delilah insisted.

"It's not going on forever. Come on…you're getting ahead of yourself."

Delilah wiped at her tears. "Yeah, well, okay. We don't know about forever. True. But still…"

Tenika stepped back to the stove for a moment and gave her braising oxtails a stir. "All we need to know is how we're getting through today, baby. Today is good enough." She glanced over her shoulder at Delilah. "That's all we've really got anyway, right?"

Delilah sat down wearily. "Yeah, I suppose. Whatever."

"Well, I know, and that's the facts, sister. We'll find a doctor. We'll get the health insurance. We'll do this thing."

"Oh!" Delilah looked up suddenly. "Rhonda gave me a check for a thousand for health insurance. It was amazing. She just handed it to me. And Rennie's going to help me find a doctor."

Tenika chuckled as she poured the rest of the chopped carrots into her stew. "Exactly what I'm talking about. We've got this. We're in flow here. Don't worry about it."

Now Delilah stood up. "But, T, I don't have my share of the rent next month...or the month after or..."

"No, but I do. That's why I've got all those savings, remember?"

Delilah sat down again. Sadly, she looked at the table. "Oh, T, honey. I *can't* wipe out your savings."

"Who says you're wiping them out? That's what they're there for, anyway."

"But they're there for you, those savings. Not for me," Delilah insisted.

Tenika just looked at her. "Who made up that rule?" Delilah just looked at her.

Walking back to her, Tenika put her hand on her chin and tipped Delilah's face towards her own. "Look, I *want* to take care of you, okay? I really do."

Looking up at her, Delilah could see T's face was washed with love and concern. "Really?"

Tenika nodded gravely. "Really."

"Okay," Delilah said in a small voice. Then she sniffed and laughed. "This is just so...wow."

"Yep. But it's life, right? We take care of each other."

"I guess so," Delilah said in mild wonder.

Tenika turned back to her stew and gave it another stir. "We're all here, waiting to help you, sister. All you have to do is say yes."

"I get it," Delilah said.

And she did.

Chapter Ten

Kate's footsteps echoed through the empty apartment. By all measures, it was perfect. Not only was it big enough and bright, it was on a quiet tree-lined street in the Laurel district. And it was well below market rate.

Granted, it was only a studio, and an illegal sublet at that, but it was enough for now. Really, Kate had no idea how she'd gotten the place.

"It's wonderful," she told the man renting it. "Completely perfect."

"Glad you like it," he smiled, handing her the contract to sign. Kate glanced through it quickly.

"It's a six-month lease," she said, looking up.

"That's right—didn't you know?"

"Oh…yes. Right," Kate demurred. Then she shook her head. "It's perfect." This explained the price, but for all she knew, six months might actually be the perfect amount of time to live here. At least by then she'd know for certain how she felt about moving back in with Lizzy.

Quickly, Kate signed the contract and handed it back to the man with a check. A moment later, he was gone and Kate stood in the middle of her space, just looking around. Hugging herself, she walked from the living/sleeping room into the tiny kitchen, and then back again.

Running her hand along the cracked trim covered with layer after layer of paint, she wondered how many other souls had lived here. And how many of them had been caught in the same sort of strangely uncomfortable in-between place.

Kate turned on the kitchen faucet, then she shut it off again. She curiously lit a few burners on the stove. Then she opened the door to the tiny refrigerator and found its lone item—a single remaining can of Pepsi.

Turning back once more to the studio, Kate imagined herself lying in bed in her own space, beneath her own comforter and her own sheets, with her own thoughts running through her own head. There would be no strange guilty sense of obedience to Mindy Rose, or the stifled sense of obligation to Lizzy. Not to mention the ever-present worry that they'd rushed their entire relationship.

Instead, it would just be Kate, living in the here and now, feeling her feelings and living her life. Making choice after choice just for herself, rediscovering her own potent power.

Kate grinned. She'd managed to get here. She'd actually done it.

This was exactly what she needed.

*

Lizzy gave her socket wrench a hard twist. Then she popped the errant lighting control module out of the Toyota she was working on. Inserting the defunct piece into the worn pocket of her blue coveralls, she pulled the new one from its box and wiggled it back into position.

Peering up into the back of the dashboard with a tiny flashlight, she fussed for a moment with the tricky piece. "Damn," she muttered as she finally finessed it into place.

A moment later, she stood wiping her hands on a rag. Then she sighed heavily.

Tenika looked over from the brake job she was working on. They were alone in the garage. "What's so heavy?" she asked.

Lizzy shook her head. "Nothing."

Tenika gave her a look. "Oh?"

"Okay, well, there's some shit going on if you really want to know."

"I do."

Lizzy paused, hands on hips. "Last night, Kate told me she's moving out."

"What?" Carefully, Tenika worked the balky rotor off the wheel mount in front of her. Then she put it down and looked at her partner. "What the fuck?"

"That's what I said."

"You guys are breaking up?" Tenika asked, but Lizzy shook her head.

"Apparently not."

"But..."

Lizzy shrugged. "But nothing. She says she needs to *choose* the relationship, whatever the hell that's supposed to mean. She needs so called 'space.'"

"Hmm," said Tenika, folding her arms. "I guess I can see her point."

"What point?" Lizzy exploded, her voice ratcheting up. "We were going along just fine, and then BOOM—suddenly she's moving out. This is like..." Lizzy slumped on a nearby stool, and her voice cracked. "It's ridiculous."

"Lizzy, it's not ridiculous," Tenika said. "At least I don't think it is."

Lizzy just stared at her business partner. "What are you talking about?"

Tenika took up a spot near Lizzy. "Listen, you've got to get out of your own head here, girl. You just do. You don't have any choice. I mean, be practical. She's going, and you're going to lose her completely if you don't step back."

Lizzy sighed heavily. "But I don't get it. I don't! What's so bad about living together?"

"In the right time and place, nothing. But she got forced into moving in with you. You know she did. And Lizzy, honey, she always said it was temporary."

Lizzy was silent. As usual, Tenika was telling the uncomfortable truth.

"I mean, I know it's hard," Tenika continued, "but you can't make her wrong for having her feelings. Kate's gonna do what Kate's gonna do, right? And you just have to go with it. If you love her…you will."

Lizzy sighed. "I don't know," she said. Uncertainty swirled around her. She really *didn't* know. It seemed highly unlikely that Kate would actually move out and still truly be her girlfriend. That part just seemed like so much lip service.

"Okay," said Tenika simply. "That's fine. Just remember—you have no control. All you can worry about is your own thing. You know what I'm saying?"

"I do. And it sucks."

"It hella sucks. But it's also the truth, and it's better to hang on to the truth than drown in a sea of lies."

Lizzy looked up. "Who said that?"

Tenika gave her a look. "I did."

"I just frigging hate not knowing what's going to happen."

"Welcome to reality, sister," Tenika said. She picked up her micrometer and began to take measurements of the worn rotor.

"Why don't you let Sally read your cards?" she continued.

"Sally, your couch surfer?"

Tenika recorded the micrometer readings. "Uh-huh."

Lizzy glanced over at her. "What? Like…Tarot cards?"

"Mmm-hmm. She's not bad. Did mine the other night, and she saw that Delilah's gonna be fine. And I believe she is."

"Well, that's cool, but honestly, T. Tarot cards?"

"She's a psychic!" Tenika said. "And a decent one. You'd be lucky to get a reading."

Lizzy shrugged. "Maybe." Once again she picked up her flashlight and peered into the inner circuitry of the Toyota's dashboard.

"You and Kate are going to be fine," Tenika announced a moment later. "You just have to speak your truth, you know? It's part of showing up."

"Well, apparently I haven't got any choice," Lizzy said.

Tenika smiled at her. "Now you're getting it," she said approvingly.

*

Delilah shifted uncomfortably on the white paper that covered the exam table. At least they weren't making her wear the requisite freezing cold gown. She looked over at Tenika. They'd been sitting there for nearly fifteen minutes. "And so we wait," she said.

"Yep. Pretty standard," Tenika agreed.

The clock on the wall ticked loudly.

"Let's go by the Yemeni place on Telegraph. Get some local raw honey. It's supposed to be good for the nervous system," Tenika said after a moment. "Anyway, I like that guy, Khaled. He speaks for the bees."

Delilah sighed. "I just want to get through this."

Just then, the door opened. A young woman in a lab coat breezed in. "Hi, I'm Dr. Desai," she said. She glanced at the open laptop on the stand by her stool. "You have a tremor," she announced, as she spread antibacterial gel on her hands. Then she smiled perkily at Delilah. "Let's have a look."

Delilah and Tenika exchanged glances as Dr. Desai scanned Delilah's chart online. "You haven't had a general workup?" she asked, looking up in wonder.

"I didn't have a doctor until now."

Dr. Desai nodded. "Ah. Well, you'll need a checkup. But meanwhile, let's look at the tremor. Hold out your hand."

Delilah held her shaking hand in front of her. "Pronounced," said the doctor. "Is it all the time or just when you're resting?" she asked.

"All the time."

She peered into Delilah's eyes with a small light. "Look here," she said, waving a finger in front of her face. After a moment, the doctor put away the instrument. "How's your sense of smell?"

"Fine," said Delilah.

The doctor led Delilah into the corridor outside the examining room and instructed her to walk up and down the hallway.

"Well, I'd say you don't have Parkinson's," she announced as they came back in the room. "What else...what else?" she muttered as she looked at the screen. "No drooling, sweating, stomach pain, heavy vomiting?" she asked.

"No," Delilah said uneasily. *Where was all this going?*

"Then you haven't been poisoned," the doctor said. Brightly, she turned to the pair. "I think we ought to refer you to a neurologist for an MRI—just to make sure you don't have a brain tumor. I'll email you a referral this afternoon," she said pleasantly.

Then, in a flash, the doctor was gone.

Delilah and Tenika looked at each other.

"Shit," Delilah said.

"Yup," Tenika agreed.

Suddenly, the entire idea of taking spoonfuls of local raw honey seemed ridiculous. At least it did if Delilah had a brain tumor, and the only way out of that was surgery. Like...serious life-altering surgery. On her brain.

"Fuck," said Delilah. Wearily, she stood up. An MRI was not what she was counting on at all.

"Let's go home, baby," said Tenika, holding out her hand. "I'm taking the rest of the afternoon off."

Delilah nodded, reaching for Tenika's warm, steady hand. She was immensely glad she wasn't alone.

*

Mindy settled her pink Kate Spade bag on top of the stack of files and electronics in her lap. She wanted to be as prepared as possible for her first meeting with the new immigration lawyer.

She smiled a bright smile of hope at the man in front of her. "So?" she said. "Where would you like me to begin?"

The gray-haired lawyer on the opposite side of the table rearranged his tie over his slightly expansive gut, took up his pen, and prepared to make notes on the yellow pad in front of him. "Start at the beginning, Ms. Rose," he said, nodding.

"Call me Mindy," she said with a nose wrinkle. "Well, the issue is Kate Morahan, an illegal alien who I happen to know is working illegally in Oakland. I'd like to get her deported."

The attorney looked up and put his pen down. "This is not about your own immigration status?"

"Me? Heavens no," Mindy said. "I'm an American, born and raised."

The attorney sat back and looked at her with interest. "Continue."

"Well, Kate's an illegal. That's all you really need to know, right? We have to get her out of here."

"Undocumented worker is the preferred phrase, Ms. Rose," the lawyer said. Then he looked at her a little distastefully. "Has this woman done anything to cause you particular concern?"

Mindy shifted in her seat and gave a derisive laugh. "What hasn't she done?" she asked. "She tried to shut down my business. She's threatened me. And then she quit!"

The attorney blinked. "Quit?"

"She worked for me for seven years," Mindy explained.

The attorney gave a half smile and stared at his notepad. Then he looked up at her, trying to keep a straight face. "Ms. Rose, I need to point out to you that you, yourself, employed this woman. You have also been breaking the law."

Mindy closed her half-opened mouth and glanced uncomfortably at the stack of paraphernalia in her lap. "I don't care," she suddenly announced. "She's illegal, and I want her gone."

The attorney glanced out the window. Then he looked back at her intensely. "Look, I don't do revenge cases," he said. "Especially when I can't explain to the U.S. government why my client was illegally hiring undocumented workers herself."

"Fine," said Mindy, standing up with a lurch. She clutched at her files. "Fine!" she repeated. Turning on her kitten heel, she stomped towards the door and yanked the doorknob open. Then she glanced over her shoulder. "I hate people like you," she announced. "All high-minded and…whatever!" Dramatically, Mindy then made her exit.

One way or another, she'd get rid of Kate. Even if she had to do it herself.

*

"Kennedy, I've had enough for one day, so make it short." Wearily, the Lieutenant returned to the stack of papers on his desk. He refused to even look at Frankie.

Meanwhile, Frankie was doing her best to show up as trustworthy. Promotion-worthy, even.

"Look, I get that. I understand, Lieutenant. I'm just saying it's not my fault the perp's car got burned. It was totally the patrol cop who did it, not us. We were practically ready to do the raid. We knew where the suspect lived. We'd done the entire risk assessment to the letter. We had the team in place, but there was some nonsense with his registration. Next thing we knew this patrol dude is pulling the guy over. Then he didn't even detain him! Perp's probably in L.A. by now, and we have to start all over again. Need I say more?"

The Lieutenant stopped his paperwork and looked at her blankly. He was not amused. "Can't help you," he said gruffly. Then he moved on to the next document in the stack, busying himself elsewhere.

Still Frankie just sat there. She would leave if she could think where to go next, or what to do. At this moment, everything felt hopeless.

The Lieutenant finally looked up at her. "Kennedy. What did I just say?"

Finally, she stood up. "Okay. Okay! Sorry. I just..." Words failed her. What she really wanted right now was to ask him for something, but exactly how—or even what—was not clear to her. The failed surveillance job was only the excuse that got her there.

Frankie actually had bigger things on her mind. "Here's the thing, Lieutenant," she began.

He looked up once more in annoyance and tapped his pen on the desktop. "Kennedy, we're done. What are you not getting here?"

It's not actually about that, she wanted to say. Instead, self-preservation stopped her. There was no way in hell she could go to her immediate superior about her creeping case of PTSD. Not when she'd only been plainclothes for less than six months.

It just wasn't done, and certainly not when you were one of the few women who served that district.

Frankie exhaled. "Okay. Okay, fine," she said, rising and turning to go.

Today was not the day. Tomorrow wouldn't be either. Who knew when the right time would be.

Never, maybe.

As she walked out of the station, Frankie pulled out her phone and glanced at it. There was a call from an unknown number. It had an Oakland area code. Frankie studied it for a moment curiously.

Who was calling her from the East Bay?

A text popped in from the same number. "Hi. This is Sally, Lizzy and Kate's friend. Would you like to chat?"

Sally. Frankie half smiled. Good, she needed a distraction from the day from hell. It would be all too easy right now to sit around and fume about how a good three weeks of work had just been shot to hell.

"I'll text you a little later," she typed. Then shoving the phone in her pocket, she smiled to herself.

It was probably a little too soon to give up altogether, wasn't it?

Chapter Eleven

Kate pulled open the drawer to the old oak bureau and examined the contents. It hadn't been that long since she and Lizzy had found it on Craig's List, driven over to Berkley, and bought it from the young hetero couple who were moving out.

She could clearly remember Lizzy's smile of satisfaction as they wrapped it carefully in blankets and loaded it into the back of her truck. Lizzy had even offered to refinish it, but Kate declined, which was probably the first sign that this living together experiment of theirs was temporary.

Sadness flooded her now. This was not how she wanted to live, with one foot in a serious relationship and the other foot inching rapidly out the door. Here she was, actually taking steps to leave. Yet, she knew she was far from quitting Lizzy.

She stood looking at her underwear and socks for a moment. Giving up on Lizzy now would be tantamount to giving up on life. It was all too aligned. Too right. At least that's how it seemed most of the time…until she felt the sudden urge to withdraw.

What was wrong with her anyway?

Kate gently closed the drawer. Then she sat down on their bed and sighed. A deep sense of shame filled her like a cloud of toxic smoke. This was not good.

Breathing in, Kate reminded herself once again it was actually okay to step back and take some time for herself. If nothing else, she knew she needed it, no matter how scared she was. She thought, then, about the excitement she'd felt only the day before, walking through the empty apartment and handing over the first and last month's rent and the security deposit. And getting the keys in her hand.

The keys to a place of her own.

That payment had nearly cleaned out her bank account. Yet, even this quickly resolved itself, as well. The first payment from her new winery client happened to be waiting for her as soon as she got home.

Really, the entire thing had unfolded in such a natural, easy way. As if it truly were meant to be. The only hiccup—well, major impediment, really—was the tormented face of Lizzy when Kate told her she was leaving. And then the way she took off in the night on her bike.

Lizzy only did that when things were really intense.

Kate hated that stab of hurt. Lizzy's displeasure crawled inside her skin and made her feel deeply ashamed of herself. Yet, she could not have it both ways. She either left and pursued this space she felt she needed, or she stayed, committed completely to her relationship and pushing away her own thoughts and needs.

Kate closed her eyes. She could hear Lizzy moving around in the other room. Lizzy had been quiet since Kate told her about the new apartment. Neither surly nor indifferent, she'd just been sad. And true to form, Kate could feel it.

Still, heartbreakingly, Lizzy had offered to help her move three times in the last 24 hours.

"I know you need to leave, and okay, I don't like it," she told Kate. "But I'm not fighting it anymore, either. Just let me help you."

Of course, Kate agreed, for how could she say no? Yet, the idea of Lizzy patiently carrying her bureau up the stairs to the new studio was nearly as painful as telling her she was leaving in the first place.

It was that damn poignancy again. If only she could stop feeling every last modicum of Lizzy's pain.

Now Lizzy appeared in the doorway. "Hi," she said. Lizzy paused in the doorway and leaned against it.

"Hi."

Lizzy folded her arms and looked at Kate. "Just wondered what you're doing."

Kate smiled up at her. "Oh, just…things. I don't know."

Lizzy sighed and looked at her boots. There was a long, awkward silence. "I'm really okay with it," Lizzy announced after a moment. "You leaving and everything. I mean, you've got to do what you've got to do, right? And I don't *understand* it. I mean, I really, really don't. But I accept it." She paused. "Reluctantly."

Kate nodded. "Thanks," she said.

Another awkward pause ensued.

"Anyway, I guess I'd better go," Lizzy stammered.

"Okay."

She stayed in the doorway a moment longer. The two women exchanged a long look. "Okay," Lizzy finally said. "See you later."

"Yes. See you later."

Then, finally, Lizzy was gone. Kate stood up and took a deep breath. Opening the drawer once again, she began to remove the small tidy piles of clothing in front of her, placing them in her waiting suitcase.

This was going to be harder than she thought.

*

Lizzy coasted down the hill on Allendale towards High Street, pumping the bike brakes just enough on her way to rehearsal. Her blues band, The Breakdowns, was a godsend at moments like this. All she needed to do was get going on a guitar solo, or lose herself in singing one of their old soul classics, and hope would once again appear.

Still, at this moment, Lizzy's mind raced and she gripped the brake handles tighter and tighter. Finally, at the end of the hill, her bicycle screeched to a halt.

For a moment, Lizzy just sat there, stock still.

Anger, frustration, and hurt clouded her head. She clenched her teeth together, trying not to feel the old echoes of an ancient pain in her body. Lizzy knew that everything Kate was saying was reasonable and fair. Kate was, indeed, entitled to step away and find her way back to the relationship on her own terms.

It was only right she try living on her own for a while. Wasn't it?

One small tear of betrayal inched down her cheek, and Lizzy wiped it away with annoyance. She seriously hated her life at this moment. Mainly because this was what always happened. Even after so many years and so many relationships, she always managed to wind up resolutely alone.

And man, she didn't want to be.

No, Lizzy was a fighter. So fight she would—for living together, or against uncertainty. Or even just for the idea that they made sense as a committed couple.

Lizzy was also a romantic. She really believed in "the one," and that one day, when she finally met this mythic soulmate, she would know it in her soul. There would really be that destined eternal sense of rightness. This time she'd been 100% sure she felt it with Kate. Lizzy had felt sure, like she never had before. So it became all Kate, all the time, right from the beginning.

But now, here they were on the verge of breaking up.

Lizzy shrugged the guitar case on her back more securely into place. Then she blew her nose and set off again, pumping slowly.

How could they have found their way here? She'd never felt this way before. Not once. Not with any of the others. With Kate, there was always a sense of unbridled possibility. There was honest to God hope. There was instant connection. And there wasn't even the slightest shadow of a doubt.

There was also the kind of electric, stratospheric sex that stood in a class of its own. Only two people who were destined to be together could make love like this, Lizzy reasoned.

Still, there was also the challenge of luring Kate in and holding her fast. For although Kate talked about commitments, she always managed to slip away somehow. Lizzy reflected on this as she rode on.

There was the time they were down in that B&B in Monterey, lying in bed in the late morning. The sun was painted across their bodies as they lay there in their warm, apres-sex emptiness. They'd made love for hours that morning, and now they were left both exhausted and energized.

That morning, Lizzy had assumed they would be together forever, and she even said something to that effect. Immediately, Kate disagreed.

"Oh, Lizzy, you can't go on like that," she cautioned. "We may be dead tomorrow."

Lizzy could still remember the sting Kate's words had left. Just one moment earlier, she felt strong, free, full of the gift of life, and so grateful for everything she knew her lover to be.

Then, in an instant, all of that suddenly vanished.

So here she was again, feeling as alone and vulnerable as she ever had been. It was such a familiar place. Tenika's words in the garage came back to her: *Living with Kate was just meant to be temporary.*

Lizzy shook her head, as if trying to fling the hard truth right out of existence. She was so tired of being alone—so very, very tired of it. Why couldn't Kate be the one? Why couldn't she just move in and stay put? What was so very wrong with that?

Lizzy pulled up to a stoplight and waited for it to change.

The problem, of course, was that she wanted control. And she wanted to pre-work the damage control before Kate even had a chance to think about moving out.

And now…well…here she was.

Again.

So much for that strategy, Lizzy thought with dismay.

On the other hand, she reasoned, if she just cut the cord—if she really let Kate go, no questions asked—then perhaps this soul-mate-to-be really would come back to her.

Either way, at least she'd finally know the truth about how Kate really felt. After all, Kate said she didn't want to break up. So maybe she didn't.

Lizzy pumped on as the light turned green. She had a long way to go to willingly give up Kate. But perhaps the choice really wasn't hers to begin with.

Maybe it never had been.

*

Frankie stared ahead at the traffic desert ahead. Bumper to bumper, the cars inched forward into the perpetual glaring sun of another Bay Area Wednesday evening. It really had been a crap day. Only the possibility of a chat with the new, potentially interesting Sally seemed to lighten things up.

Frankie rotated her shoulders as she sat there, trying unsuccessfully to release the locked-up tension in her body. She looked down at the phone as it buzzed. A number with an unfamiliar area code was calling her.

Good. Sally was calling her back.

"Hello?" she said, trying to muster her best neutral but friendly voice.

"Hi. It's Sally. Kate's friend." The voice on the other end was gentle. Unassuming.

"Oh…yeah. Hi."

"Hi," Sally repeated. There was a pause.

"How's your day going?" Frankie asked, for lack of something better to say. Really, she'd never been good at this sort of thing, but at least she was trying.

"My day?" Sally gave a small laugh. "Well, perfectly lovely, thank you. Every day is completely different at this moment in my life, and I've learned to say yes to them all. You know," she paused. "You can't really fight, right?"

Frankie smiled. "Ain't that the truth?" she said. Then she paused. Sally sounded philosophical. "So can you spread a little of that optimistic world view over here on 580? We're at a standstill here."

Sally chuckled. "I've been talking to the traffic gods, Frankie, and they're seriously pissed."

Frankie grinned again. She had no idea who this woman was, but she was already intrigued. "Oh yeah?"

"They keep trying to train us all to walk and ride bikes. But do we listen? No!"

"Believe me, I would if I could," Frankie replied. Then she steeled herself, expecting the inevitable. This was the moment when she'd have to start lying about what she did. But that moment didn't actually arrive. Instead, Sally moved on smoothly without missing a beat.

Interesting. Frankie straightened up slightly in her seat.

"How's your day going?" Sally asked now.

Frankie paused, not wanting to be the big heavy on the call. Not now—not with this new, unknown quantity named Sally. "Oh…it was just another day," she said. "Check. Done."

"Ah. So you're a person who likes to get things done?"

"Aren't we all?"

"Not necessarily. I think doing stuff is overrated," Sally said. "You get to the end of your life and then what do you have?"

"Uh…accomplishment?"

"Perhaps. But what about all the things you missed?"

"Like?"

"Like relationships—and rosebuds, and seascapes, and old Joni Mitchell records. And rainbows and unicorns."

"Yeah, let's hear it for rainbows and unicorns," Frankie chimed in, for lack of anything better to say.

"And children, of course," Sally continued. "I don't have any kids. Do you?"

Frankie practically choked. "No. I don't," she said. "I was never interested."

"Yeah. I haven't gotten around to it either," Sally remarked. "But you have to admit they can be pretty cute. Just today I was sitting on a bench near a playground, and a toddler tried to give me her plastic shovel. She honestly wanted me to sit down in her sandbox and play with her. Here I was, a total stranger. And you know, I did for a while. She was the most enchanting little person."

There was a silence. Frankie couldn't tell if this woman was for real. And was this some veiled early play for raising children? If so…what was up with that? "So what sort of work do you do, Sally?" Frankie asked. The conversation needed to get back to neutral territory.

"Oh, this and that…different things." Sally's voice grew quieter.

"Like what sort of things?"

Sally chuckled. "You can go first on that one, Frankie."

Screw it. Frankie was tired of waiting for some perfect woman to land in her life. Now was the time to at least make a move. Sally sounded good enough. Desirable, even. For one thing, she was clearly a positive person. And she sounded so calm and relaxed.

On the other hand, she could have a record. Or maybe Sally was a con artist. Frankie found herself shaking her head. There was no way in hell. This was a perfectly decent woman.

And…they still hadn't met. There might not be one iota of chemistry. Still, Frankie reasoned. It was worth a shot.

"Do you want to have dinner?" she asked Sally. "Maybe Friday night?"

"Sure," Sally said with the air of someone who didn't even need to look at her calendar. It occurred to Frankie briefly that she might be homeless, or at least unemployed. She shooed away this very inconvenient thought and set to booking their date.

A few moments later it was done, and their conversation ended. For all she knew, Sally really could work in a java bar, unlike Tasha who only pretended to. But at this point, that was even preferable.

In Sally's voice was all the hope and optimism Frankie had been craving. It was the sound of possibility. Delight, even. Clearly, Sally was a happy person, and somehow that was all that mattered now.

Frankie smiled to herself as the traffic ahead finally began to move.

*

Well, that was refreshing.

Sally smiled as she put the phone back into her backpack. Who knew what this Frankie character was all about. Still, it felt strangely good to talk to her.

There wasn't much one could tell from a mere phone call. Sally knew this, of course. Really, she was still back on the larger question of whether she was even ready to date again so soon. Wasn't she still technically grieving her breakup with girlfriend number twelve?

She could hear her friend Brian's voice in her ear: "You can still grieve and date at the same time." She smiled. Ever the optimist, that Brian.

As she sat there on a sunny bench by Lake Merritt, the possibility of a new relationship seemed distant and a little surreal. Still, some things were fated, and Sally was never one to rock the karmic boat. And she did, indeed, have a very particular feeling about Frankie.

She'd felt it the moment she heard Frankie's voice on the phone. Certainty landed for her like a heavy rock plunging into a deep well. It was that silent sense that the two of them were not only meant to cross paths, but to build something together.

It would be big, she thought. Bigger than anything either of them had known before.

Sally breathed in the afternoon and stretched in the languor of her bench. She'd had an interesting day, full of signposts and portent. Only an hour earlier, she'd stopped to help a broken old man who'd dropped his glasses on the sidewalk. She came upon him just as he was bent over, scrounging for the glasses that his shaking hand could barely reach.

Reaching over easily, Sally scooped up the glasses and handed them to the old man. He took them with a nod and shuffled off, and she watched him go for a moment. Then she happened to glance over and take in the store she was standing in front of.

Desire's Magical Garden read the sign.

Immediately, Sally wondered why she hadn't noticed it before. Stepping closer, she peered in the window. A tall wooden figurine of the goddess of compassion, Kwan Yin, placidly gazed back at her. Surrounding the statue was a panoply of crystals, candles, rocks, feathers, sacred stones, wands, and various bits of ephemera. Here was all the arcane accoutrement of the well-fitted spiritual but not religious altar. A white laughing Buddha sat at Kwan Yin's feet, just beside an array of tiny bronze goddesses.

Sally was immediately intrigued. She tried the handle of the door, but it was locked. It appeared the store was closed.

She peered inside. Well past the endless display cases of crystals, stones, books, and assorted figurines was a small darkened room. Its entrance was festooned with a parted heavy velvet curtain. A red-winged Balinese dragon soared just above the doorway. This was the Hindu guardian Busuki, clearly there to chase away any bad spirits who wandered in.

Sally smiled to herself when she saw this. Someone at Desiree's Magical Garden knew just what they were doing. For in this tiny room, psychic readings were undoubtedly being given. A discreet sign in the front window said as much.

At the time, Sally had regarded the place curiously. Now as she thought about it, Sally leaned back against her bench by the lake and enjoyed the warm, sunny breeze as it landed on her skin. She would have to go back, of course.

Perhaps this would even be her next landing spot.

Chapter Twelve

"Nice afternoon," Sally remarked as she climbed out of Delilah's car. The two women surveyed the broad dirt path that began just ahead of them. Then they looked at each other and smiled.

The East Ridge was an easy ramble up and down the wild rolling Bay Area hills, and it felt a million miles from the city. To their right, a panoramic layer cake of hills, ridges, and trees in varying shades of green, brown, and gray extended to the horizon. Redwood Regional Park was the perfect place to leave your tension on a Friday afternoon.

"I'd forgotten about this place," Delilah said as they began to walk. "I'm glad you thought of it."

Sally smiled. "Me, too. I love it up here."

They walked in silence for a while, passing dog walkers and runners. A trio of giggling teenage girls hurried past, trying to keep up with an unruly sheepdog who was bounding ahead of them.

"So how are things?" Delilah began.

"Fine," Sally said, and she meant it. "I have no complaints. Got a blind date tonight."

Delilah glanced at her. "Really? So soon?"

Sally shrugged. "I'm not sure if I'm ready to date anyone. But it's just a little dinner. We'll see."

"And?" Delilah looked at her friend knowingly.

Sally blushed a bit and looked at the ground with a smile. "And nothing."

Delilah stopped cold and looked at her friend. "You so got a hit on this. Look at you. You're practically oozing pheromones."

Sally nodded. "Yeah, well…okay. There's probably something there, but who am I to say? At least that's what I get. But maybe it's nothing." She glanced at her friend a little helplessly. "I'm trying to stay grounded here."

Delilah laughed. "Well, okay! Just don't get too carried away, yeah?"

Sally shook her head and sighed. "Like I have a choice?" she asked. She looked at her friend with mild exasperation. "I would if I could."

"Right."

They walked on in silence a bit longer. "So what about you?" Sally asked.

Delilah looked out at the path ahead of them. "Well, T and I are still together. I guess you figured that out by now. It's 'complicated' as they say."

"I live with you two, and I don't really have any idea what's going on."

Delilah glanced at her friend. "Yeah, neither do we. I mean, T swears she'd never leave me. She says she wants to take care of me no matter what happens, but we don't even know what we're dealing with here. I mean, this could be a terrible, life-altering thing, right?"

"Or it could be nothing," Sally noted.

Delilah looked at her sharply. "Are you withholding something from me?"

Sally threw up her hands. "No! No, not at all. I haven't got anything about your illness. No hits. Nothing. I just have…well, I've learned patience with things like this. You can't rush in assuming you know what's happening when you don't, right?"

"And still the question remains," Delilah said. Her voice was somber and quiet.

"Which question?"

"The one you asked me the other day. Why do I want to get married so badly? Remember?"

"Oh, yeah," Sally said, remembering their conversation. She glanced at Delilah as they walked along. "So what have you decided?"

"I've decided I have no idea. I mean, maybe marriage is just this thing that straight people cooked up to organize everyone into little boxes, married and unmarried. Maybe it's just some sort of grand scheme that society imposed." Delilah paused for a moment, surveying the horizon.

"Look at my family," she continued. "All of my sisters and brothers are married except for me. And now T and I can get married, so part of me is like, 'Why not just do it?' Then we could finally fit in and be like everyone else." Delilah stopped and glanced at her friend. "But who knows if that's even a semi-decent reason to get married. Is this making any sense?"

"Yes," Sally assured her. "Still, there is a certain unarguable aspect to marriage you can't just forget."

"Which is?"

Sally looked at her. "Love, Delilah. You can't argue with love."

Delilah glanced down and took in the space around her. "True."

"Do you love Tenika?"

Delilah looked her friend in the eye. "Yeah. I do."

"Good," Sally said. "Sounds like you're making progress."

"I guess we'll just have to wait and see," Delilah said as they picked up their pace again. "Cause if I know one thing, this tremor is kicking my ass in every possible way. And I need her. Like… seriously."

"So in the end," Sally said, "maybe the tremor's not an entirely bad thing."

Delilah looked at her friend. "Yeah," she said. "I guess."

This was exactly why Sally was living on their couch.

*

Frankie played nervously with her straw. She'd plucked it out of the whiskey and soda that had arrived a few moments earlier, and now she drummed it against the paper top on their table in the Indian restaurant.

She would never have chosen Indian. It was Sally's choice. But again, this was still the new Frankie. She was ready to enjoy her blind date as much as she could.

Now she glanced at her watch. Sally was six minutes late.

Six minutes is no big deal, she chided herself. *Just relax.*

At that moment, the chimes tied to the door to the restaurant gave an Eastern jangle as a blonde woman walked in. Immediately, Frankie knew it was Sally. She was taller than Frankie had expected, and her hair was tied with an ethereal blue and white chiffon scarf. Large silver circles with some sort of Indian symbol on them dangled from her ears. She cocked her head and looked at Frankie. "Are you…" she started to say. Then Sally flashed a smile that momentarily dazzled her.

Frankie took a quick pull of her drink for fortification. She stood up, summoning her full five foot four inches. She greeted the now fast approaching Sally.

"Hi!" she said, extending a hand then quickly withdrawing it. "Here…," Frankie stammered, heading over to pull out Sally's chair.

"I've got it," Sally said easily, waving Frankie away.

All of Frankie's lights were on and flashing. *This woman was seriously beautiful.* Even with the biggest earrings Frankie had ever seen.

They grinned at each other. "Hello!" Sally said. "I'm glad to meet you."

"Yeah! Yeah…definitely." Frankie handed over one of the bulky menus. "Would you like a drink? A chai? A cocktail? An Indian beer maybe…or a water?" Her voice gave a little squeak, and she was suddenly almost uncontrollably nervous. *Who knew this woman would be such a complete and total dish? Holy mother of God.*

Kate wasn't kidding, apparently. Frankie inhaled and focused on her menu. In an effort to calm down, she willed her breathing to slow.

"Are you okay?" Sally asked, glancing at her curiously.

"Yeah! Excellent." *Jesus! Calm the hell down,* Frankie implored herself.

Now she turned intently to the task of ordering. It seemed like the only thing she could do at this point. "So what are you in the mood for, Sally? I've never been here, but Biriyani is always good. And you can't go wrong with Chicken Tikka. Crowd pleaser, right? Then there's samosas, which are probably decent. Got to hope they're not mushy. Just hate a mushy samosa…"

Frankie realized she was rambling, so she shut her mouth and focused on her menu, but every so often, she snuck a glance across the table at Sally who was quietly absorbing the room around them. Her eyes came to rest on Frankie.

Frankie glanced away, slightly embarrassed to be caught.

"Have you been here before?" Frankie asked, eyes now fastened on her menu.

Sally shook her head and smiled placidly. "Nope. I just arrived in the East Bay, basically."

"Ah. From where?"

A waiter now appeared. "Are you ladies ready?"

"I am," Sally announced. Frankie suddenly realized she had no idea what she was going to order. Or talk about. Or anything. It was like she'd been momentarily disabled, and not because Sally was a traditional beauty. Frankie snuck another glance at her.

Some might say her hips were too curvy or even too big, or they might notice that her front teeth were just ever so slightly crooked. But when Sally laughed, which she'd done twice so far, the room lit up. No—the world lit up.

Get a freaking grip, Frankie chided herself. *You don't even know this woman. She could be anyone.*

They ordered dinner, and the waiter disappeared. "So, what do you do anyway?" Frankie began. She figured she might as well get down to it.

"I thought you were going to tell me first," Sally said with a smile.

"Okay. Here's an idea," Frankie said. "Let's not discuss that tonight. Let's just...not. Okay?"

"Fine with me," Sally shrugged. "I thought you wanted to know."

Frankie took a pull of her drink and waved the question away. "*La nuit est jeune*," she said.

"You speak French?"

"Sometimes." Frankie smiled shyly into her glass. "After a whiskey and soda usually. I mean...I really like France. Paris in particular. And I do go there from time to time. But my French. It's...*merde.*" She shook her head ruefully.

Sally chuckled and leaned in. She rested her chin in her hand and gazed a little dreamily at Frankie. "So what shall we talk about then?" She flashed another lazy smile in Frankie's direction, and Frankie felt her heart speed up.

This woman was seriously sexy.

Especially her eyes. They were large, green, and a little heavy-lidded, so they gave her this incredibly languid, exotic air. Like she was just extraordinarily calm all the time, or perhaps extraordinarily grounded.

Frankie resisted the urge to tell Sally how beautiful her eyes were. "I don't know," she said. "What do you think?"

They gazed at each other.

God, this was going well. A blind date! Who knew? Frankie again cautioned herself to rein it in.

"Let's play a game," Sally suggested.

"I like games." In fact, Frankie hadn't played a game in the last ten years. But on the other hand, that's probably something she needed to do more of, right? Play lots and lots of games. And freaking relax.

Sally's glass of chardonnay arrived, and it sat before her untouched. "You start. Tell me something you think may be true about me, and I'll tell you if you're right or wrong," she said. "Just based on first impressions."

"Okay." Frankie licked her lips. She didn't want to blow this. "But you go first."

"Alright." Sally studied Frankie. Then she grinned. "I think you're very organized."

Frankie smiled. "Well, yeah, probably. I mean not too organized, like not weirdly so. But…yeah. Reasonably so. I mean, I have all my insurance cards in my glove compartment."

Now it was her turn. Frankie sat back and gazed at her dinner companion. She took another sip of her drink. "I think your ancestors were English."

"Nope," said Sally. "Austrian and Welsh."

"Damn! Welsh. Close but no cigar."

"Give me another," Sally said. Frankie was warming up to the game now. She took a long breath.

"I think you're…" *What was she going to say now? What was neutral enough without being boring, yet not so specific as to be creepy?* She couldn't very well blurt out, "I think you're stunningly beautiful."

"Mmm?" Sally asked, waiting.

"Sorry. I think you've got…good dental hygiene." Frankie closed her eyes. *Christ! Where did that come from?*

Sally crossed her legs. "I floss," she said. "Now it's my turn."

They looked at each other again. Sally closed her eyes ever so briefly. Then her eyes flashed wide open. "I think you're worried about something that happened in the past. Maybe a trauma. A lot of trauma involving a child. And you're suffering now because of it."

Frankie sat up slightly. She said nothing. *What the fuck?*

Instantly, Sally realized her mistake. She looked at Frankie with alarm. "Wait! I'm sorry—forget I said that."

Frankie looked down at the table, eyebrows raised. "I think we're done with the game," she said to the tablecloth. Anxiously she glanced around the room, looking for the waiter.

Sally looked urgently across the table. "Yes, of course. Frankie, I'm sorry. I didn't need to..."

"Don't worry about it," Frankie interrupted. She tried to wave off her concern, but now all of her senses were on high alert.

Who the hell was this woman anyway?

Sally was absolutely right. Someone must have told her. But who knew about her PTSD? Nobody, that's who. Not even a therapist because Frankie hadn't been to one yet.

Still...people at work were always watching her. It was easy to say any cop could have PTSD. This woman could be a plant. But who would set her up?

Silently, Frankie stirred her drink and considered the possibilities. There were plenty on the force who didn't like women like Frankie. Maybe someone was trying to get inside her head. Force her to take early retirement.

Frankie drained the rest of her drink in one long swallow.

Was her condition that obvious?

*

Forty-five minutes later, Sally was walking home alone.

She was never going to get this right, this dating thing. She was hopelessly flawed when it came to the realities of life on earth, and she knew it. At this moment, Sally felt like crying.

Frankie was, of course, entirely her type. The minute she laid eyes on her, she'd known it. But then, when she saw all of Frankie's trauma and she dared to mention it, her date pretty much disappeared. They made banal conversation until the waiter brought their dinner, which they ate quickly and in semi-silence. Then they said goodnight.

Date over. A bust.

Now Sally was walking home alone, yet again, prisoner to the angels in her head who couldn't keep their mouths shut no matter what she did.

Yet behind her sadness, another stronger emotion prevailed. It was, improbably, hope. For if Sally were to tell the complete and total truth, she would admit the rest of what she'd seen.

She and Frankie were meant to build something powerful together. Something real. Something unexpected but great. So there was no reason to despair, and certainly not yet.

Their waltz had only just begun.

*

Lizzy moved up the stairs of Kate's new apartment, carrying the last big suitcase. Really, she didn't have much. Just a bureau, a couple of bags, and a used IKEA couch they'd found on Craig's List and hauled over in the back of the truck.

A mattress and box spring were arriving later in the afternoon. Then Kate had to go find sheets, and dishes, and...

Suddenly, the import of what she'd just done hit her as she watched her girlfriend move up the stairs silently. Stoically. For a moment, she was overwhelmed.

Lizzy put the suitcase down in the living room with a thud. "Where do you want this?" she asked.

"The bedroom is fine."

Kate watched Lizzy head off in that direction, rolling the bag behind her. She surveyed the empty expanse of the apartment around her. It was devoid of everything: rugs, curtains, prints on the walls. Even dishes and toilet paper.

Why was she actually doing this?

Kate's footsteps echoed as she walked across the room to look out the window. She inhaled, trying to calm her racing mind as she gazed into the neighbor's yard. Once again, she remembered. She was doing this for herself.

In a few moments, Lizzy would leave. The door would close. And her new phase of independence would begin.

Lizzy now returned. She walked over to Kate and stood beside her, arms folded and hands tucked up tight into her armpits. "So..." she said slowly.

Kate turned to her and put her hand on her arm. "I just want you to know I'm scared, Lizzy. I'm really scared."

Lizzy's face softened as she looked at Kate, and she sighed. Shaking her head, she could say nothing.

"And I am sorry to disappoint you," Kate continued. "I know you don't like any of this. But you've got to trust me on this, Lizzy. It's going to help us in the long run."

"So you say," Lizzy said, looking at the floor. Then she glanced up sharply at Kate. "But just do me a favor, okay?"

"Anything."

"Tell me the truth. Don't candy coat this. I need to know what's really happening."

"I am telling you the truth," Kate said.

Lizzy held her gaze for a long moment, and Kate felt herself lift up in love once more. The full impact Lizzy had had on her the first time they met swam up inside her once more. Maybe it was cell memory, or reflex. Or maybe it was some kind of ancient karmic bond. Whatever it was, she felt it now.

A pull that was strong and undeniable. It nearly took Kate's breath away.

Why was she doing this again?

"Call me," she told Lizzy. "Call me a lot."

Lizzy nodded. Then she took her in her arms at that moment and kissed her deeply. And Kate surrendered to the power of her lips, her tongue, her body holding her strong. This was too great to ignore, this thing they had. This G-force of complete and utter love.

Kate pulled back and looked into Lizzy's face, searching it for the answer. "You will, won't you?" she asked.

Lizzy shook her head helplessly. "Of course I will. I have to."

"And we can have dinner soon, alright?" Kate said and Lizzy nodded.

Slowly, she let go of Kate and took a breath. Running the back of her hand against a tear that had suddenly appeared, she sniffed hard and pulled herself up. "Okay," she said, putting her hands in her pockets.

Lizzy blew her nose in her bandanna, and then she was gone. Kate listened to Lizzy's boots rattle down the stairs.

Why on earth am I doing this?

Chapter Thirteen

The neurologist, a fifty-something preppy looking man with salt and pepper hair, hurried into the room and gave them a cursory glance. Instead of the usual official white coat, he was wearing a plaid shirt and khakis. A cord with a pair of reading glasses hung around his neck.

"Dr. Owens," he said brusquely. "Who's the patient?"

"She is," Tenika said, nodding towards her partner.

Dr. Owens hunkered down at the computer for a moment, reading Delilah's charts. He regarded her a few times across the room, then he came over to examine her. "How are you doing?" he asked. There was a small trace of medical compassion in his voice.

"Basically freaked out," Delilah said.

He nodded. "Tremors are more common than you think. Why don't you show me?"

She held out her shaking hand, and he took it, examining her fingers and her palm.

"Resting and while moving?" he asked, and she nodded.

"Looks okay here," he murmured, as he peered into her eyes with a light. Then the doctor began a series of questions. Did she have trouble talking or swallowing, involuntary movements, or a swollen abdomen? Was there a family history of Wilson's disease or tremors in general? Did she use Ritalin or cocaine? Had she had a stroke lately?

The list of questions went on and on.

Finally, after watching Delilah walk up and down the hall, count backwards, and perform several more small motor tests, the doctor appeared satisfied. "It's not Parkinson's or Wilson's disease. But you don't have tremors in the family, so we will have to look at your brain. Just to rule out MS, brain lesions, tumors, that sort of thing."

"What about MS?" asked Delilah. "Do you think I have it?"

The doctor shrugged. "We won't know for sure until we take a look."

Delilah swallowed and looked at Tenika, who shifted in her chair.

Now Tenika sat forward and addressed the doctor directly. "You sure you have to do that, doc? Like totally sure? There isn't some other way?"

He nodded. "It's just an MRI. You make an appointment. They can take care of you right here in the hospital. Your insurance will cover it. Marianne will be in shortly to do some blood work as well."

The doctor made a few notes on her chart, then rising, he prepared to leave. "The attendant will set you up with an appointment for the MRI. And really...don't worry. We do them all the time."

He disappeared now, and the two women were left sitting there, processing his information. Delilah pulled her sweater closer around her. "Can we just get out of here?" she asked in a small voice, and Tenika nodded.

"Totally."

Delilah glanced at her partner.

Now Tenika looked completely and thoroughly scared.

*

Mindy Rose sat in her car, eyeing the Driven garage just down the block. The last time she'd been here, the Black woman who co-owned the garage with Lizzy had hustled her right out of there. And forcefully.

Mindy wasn't up for a repeat performance. Which is why only moments earlier she'd done a stealth drive by the garage to see if she could spot Tenika working. There'd been no sign of her.

Mindy drew herself up and took a few sharp inhales for courage. Then she got out of the car, slammed the door shut behind her, and advanced on Driven. She was going to give Lizzy a piece of her mind.

A moment later, Mindy stalked through the open door of the garage. "Hello, Lizzy. We need to talk," she announced in a loud voice.

Lizzy was tinkering with the underside of a Prius on the lift above her, and she glanced over. Lizzy paused for a moment and took in her visitor. "Mindy Rose."

"I've reported you for hiring illegal aliens," Mindy bluffed. "Just so you know."

Given that neither the Department of Immigration and Customs Enforcement nor the Department of Homeland Security seemed to be doing much to ruffle Kate's feathers, Mindy had decided to do the job herself.

"Anyway, they're going to shut you down," she lied. Lizzy folded her arms, just listening.

Mindy circled the garage, hands on her hips, eyeing the place. "Jesus! Just look at this place. You can try to fix it up and have your little Koffee Klatch or whatever the hell that is supposed to be over there, but it won't make a bit of difference. Not when ICE drops by and closes you down."

Lizzy looked at Mindy wearily. "Are you seriously threatening me?"

"You're goddamn right I am. If you think you can steal my assistant and get away with it, you're wrong."

Lizzy sighed. "Mindy, you fired her."

"She quit! She quit to go work for you. So fuck you, Lizzy. You are trying to ruin my business."

Lizzy picked up her wrench again, making ready to return to the Prius. "Mindy, you fired her, and you know it. Anyway, she worked for you illegally. Aren't you worried about that little detail getting back to ICE?"

Mindy let out a piercing laugh. "You have to be kidding!"

"Think about it. You can't turn someone else in for employing an undocumented worker if you did it yourself for seven years."

Mindy crossed her arms. "Well, listen up, Miss Goodie Two Shoes. Don't even think about reporting me because I have a lawyer who can crush you beneath his heel. Anyway, I will simply lie. Then this shop is going to get closed right down. And you know what? I'll be believed because people love me."

"What the fuck are you doing here?"

Mindy Rose turned with a start. Seemingly out of nowhere, Tenika appeared. She began advancing rapidly on Mindy.

"I was just leaving," Mindy said, pushing towards the door. Tenika kept on coming. A few seconds later, she hurried up the sidewalk towards a quickly retreating Mindy. Then she stopped, hands on hips.

Tenika watched Mindy hustle away. A moment later, Mindy's car squealed out of her parking spot.

"That woman's sick," Tenika said when she returned. "Did I hear that correctly? Is she threatening us?"

Lizzy glanced over from the undercarriage of the Prius. "She thinks she can close us down by reporting us to ICE for hiring Kate."

"Of course she does," Tenika muttered.

Lizzy was still amazed. "She says she'll lie if we challenge her."

"Well, duh. What else is she going to say? She's got some fucking nerve."

"She can't do that," Lizzy asserted. Then she turned to her partner uncertainly. "Can she?"

Tenika shrugged. "Damned if I know. All we can do is get some proof that Kate worked for her, which shouldn't be too hard. The woman is plastered all over the media, and she's been trying to get us closed down for months. Let me see what I can find."

Lizzy put down the tool in her hand and rubbed her eyes. "I have a massive headache."

Tenika shot her partner a look. "I feel you. But at least Delilah doesn't have Parkinson's or Wilson's disease."

"Hey, that's excellent news! So now what?"

"Pictures of her brain."

"Jesus."

"Yup." Tenika stepped into her coveralls. "I hate this fucking shit. And now we have Mindy showing up, making trouble again."

"We'll deal. I'm not worried."

Tenika flipped through the list of jobs on a clipboard on the counter. "Yeah. Agreed. So how are you doing anyway?"

Lizzy shrugged. "Getting by," she said.

Tenika observed her old friend. "As in, just barely getting by."

"Basically." Lizzy cleared her throat as she tugged on an errant piece of brake lining overhead. "But I know one thing for sure," she said.

"What's that?"

Lizzy gave a final tug, and the lining came free in her hand. She popped it into the bin of garage refuse behind her, then she put her hands on her hips and regarded Tenika.

"I'll do whatever it takes to protect Kate. Even if she doesn't want to live with me. I mean…I have to, you know?"

Tenika nodded her approval. "That's good," she said. "That's real good. That's how it's supposed to be."

Lizzy nodded wordlessly and reached for a new brake lining.

The truth had just been spoken.

*

Frankie rolled over and glanced at the clock. Glaring red digital numbers informed her it was just past three o'clock in the morning. She was due to get up in 45 minutes. Work started in a little more than two hours. Exhaustion settled over her like a damp fog.

She seriously did not want to be awake right now.

Frankie gave her pillow a few pounds, and then she curled into a ball on her side. She closed her eyes with new resolve. She would go back to sleep. She could do this. And she would immediately forget about the nightmare that had just woken her.

A moment passed, and then another. But still, the dream remained. As usual, the dead child's eyes stared at her lifelessly, this time from the apartment bathtub filled with blood. This time the blood kept pouring out of the faucets of the tub, and the tub was seriously overflowing so Frankie herself was soon knee-deep in a brilliant crimson pool of blood.

As usual, it was the same girl. The one Frankie could never erase from her mind.

Fenix, Tiffany. Age 12. Female, Caucasian.

How many times was she going to have to go through this? Tiffany Fenix was only another of the many bodies she'd come upon in her line of work. Just another stiff, right? She didn't have to do anything about it, and she seriously didn't need therapy.

Tiffany's father was an abuser who went on to get life at Folsom. Justice was served. So what was the big problem here?

Turning in the other direction with a flop, Frankie closed her eyes more tightly and again attempted to sleep. Still her mind raced. She thought about the latest thing she'd read online. Recurring dreams like this were an obvious and clear symptom of PTSD.

For the forty-fifth time, she replayed her date with Sally. Everything had been going so well. At least until Sally dropped her little bomb.

"I think you're worried about something that happened in the past. Maybe a trauma. A lot of trauma involving a child. And you're suffering now because of it."

Frankie rolled onto her back. Sally had to be undercover, herself. Or…FBI? But why? What had Frankie done? Exactly nothing. So why would there be a sting on her?

Unless she'd been framed. Unless some homophobic, sadistic SOB in the higher-ups decided she had to go down. Or maybe they all knew she had PTSD, and she was the last to get it. Maybe Sally was from HR, or the union, or…well, who knew what? Maybe they were trying to get her to quit before she reached retirement.

Frankie stopped herself. This was irrational. There was no sting out there, no secret recordings, and Sally was probably not some higher-up out to entrap her. Sally was just…well, what?

Hyper-hyper-intuitive? Like crazily so?

Frankie gave up and opened her eyes. She looked at the clock. There were only seventeen minutes left before the alarm went off. Reaching over, she snapped on the lamp and stared at the ceiling.

She needed help.

Frankie set her jaw as she thought about it. There were therapists out there who worked with cops. Maybe it was time to finally go see one.

Today, on a break, she would try to get an appointment.

*

Day was just breaking as Sally opened her eyes to the dawn gloom of Tenika and Delilah's living room. It was night number thirty-seven on their couch. And it was now officially beyond old.

She closed her eyes, hoping for sleep, but once again, regret stopped her.

It was way too early to get into all of that, she chided herself. Still, Sally couldn't help it. Once more, she replayed the moment when her date with Frankie went straight to hell.

It was only the latest in a series of shame hits that had consumed her since her breakup with girlfriend number twelve. Gina's beefs were everyone's beefs about Sally: she couldn't put one foot in front of the other and function normally like everyone else.

For a while, Sally had figured Gina was wrong. But now, right here, smack in her face, was irrefutable evidence to the contrary. She'd managed to lose control and mortally offend a woman she didn't even know. A seriously sexy and interesting woman, whom she would have loved to date, had written her off within the first hour of their meeting.

What was wrong with her anyway? And weren't they supposed to have karma?

Sally sat up. She didn't have to get into all of this right now. She could go meditate, brew a pot of tea, or even take a sunrise walk. She really didn't have to roast on the spit of shame yet again. She sat up sleepily.

A few moments later, Sally sat cross-legged on the fat wide ottoman in front of the couch, doing her best to meditate. In front of her was a three-card spread from the well-worn deck of Goddess cards she used for guidance.

Reversed Kwan Yin, the Goddess of Compassion, and Artemis, also reversed, cautioned that she had shamed herself far too much in the past. Just as she had protected herself far too little, especially for one who was a bringer of light to others. In the final position, signaling the future, was Bast, the Goddess of Independence.

Bast, once again. Yet again, the card was reversed. On it, the Egyptian Goddess's arms were spread, and her gaze was utterly straightforward, invoking a call for Sally to stay strong and trust herself. For much as she was trying to jump start her life, she wasn't there yet.

Independence of spirit was still in short supply.

Bast now whispered in her ear as she meditated, or so Sally believed. In the swirl of her morning meditation, against the steady backdrop of the counting and breathing that kept her mind unoccupied, awareness filtered in.

She was growing and she was learning, yes. But most of all, Bast wanted her to forgive herself. Above all else, Sally was a truth teller. And truth tellers were sometimes unpopular messengers.

In a breath of understanding, Sally could instantly feel the rightness of this. Frankie knew what she had said at dinner that night was true, and Frankie didn't like it. That was all that happened.

This was the real dilemma. Sally could feel everyone's pain acutely, as the reversed Kwan Yin would indicate. Yet, she also felt strongly called to heal others even when it meant that she might be attacked or wrongly accused of malice.

Which is why she was given these tender gifts in the first place.

Bast's voice was soothing in her ear. *You have nothing to fear and you have done nothing wrong. Trust your truth. You are guided.*

A moment later, Sally opened her eyes, feeling significantly better. She might never see Frankie again, but she had undoubtedly given her plenty to think about. And perhaps that wasn't a bad thing after all.

In the end, Sally was just doing her job.

Chapter Fourteen

The therapist was strictly old school, requiring Frankie to leave a message after the beep. She'd been hoping to furtively book an appointment online, but such was not the case. Frankie hung up after recording her name and phone number. She felt strangely exposed.

Whatever. At least she did it. Who the hell knew if it would do any good anyway? Choosing a therapist was a random crapshoot, given how many eager women with MSWs and MFTs smiled out at her from the pages of Yelp! Finally, she picked an older woman who vaguely reminded her of her mother.

Frankie was skeptical. Mainly because she knew, intuitively, that most therapists couldn't possibly wrap their heads around the world of a cop. Logically, it just didn't seem possible. After all, most people couldn't.

Cops were people who either invoked fear or hatred most of the time. And that was before you started poking at the deep dark underbelly of trauma most of them carried around as a result of their everyday work.

Still, Frankie was trying.

She had to. There was simply no other way around it.

*

Berkeley Bowl was jammed. The lines at the registers extended back into the well-stocked aisles, past the expensive imported cheeses, and the copious boxes of unsweetened nut milks. They snaked past the artisan beef jerky, the vegan chocolate bars, and the shelves of impact-free detergents. Everywhere, patiently waiting people with loaded up carts and baskets studied their phones.

Which was exactly why Lizzy put the panniers on her bike on Tuesday nights and road up here instead of driving. Scoring a parking place at Berkeley Bowl usually required nothing less than heroics. She settled into one of the lines with her green plastic basket piled high, and she looked around. Discontent settled into her bones, but not because of the crowds.

Tuesday had been her grocery shopping night with Kate. And now here she was, buying turkey cold cuts for one.

Of course, Lizzy didn't have to come to Berkeley Bowl on a Tuesday night. She could have come on a Sunday afternoon or a Thursday night, but some habits were difficult to break. Especially when they had been hardwired with love.

Lizzy advanced a foot in the line and shoved her basket along with the toe of her boot. She folded her arms and looked around, trying to ignore the emptiness that rose up inside of her.

Her last conversation with Kate had left her craving connection. Before she called Kate, she'd already made the decision not to tell her that Mindy had shown up at the garage. That would just worry Kate, perhaps even provoking her to do something rash, like call Mindy out.

Honestly, Lizzy had no idea what Kate would do about this once she found out. Still it seemed best for now to handle things herself. Mostly, she couldn't bear the idea that Kate would sit by herself in her half-empty studio and worry. She hated the thought of Kate lying alone in her bed at night, unable to sleep.

Leave the sleeplessness for me, Lizzy decided. She would protect this woman, no matter what it took. Just like she told Tenika she would. After all, they were still together. Technically. Even though they'd only spoken once or twice since Kate left. They were even going on a date in a few days.

"Lizzy."

It was Kate's voice.

Looking up from her reverie, Lizzy glanced around, unsure where her voice was coming from. But then, there she was. Kate had just joined the line next to hers, green basket in hand.

"Hey!" Immediately, Lizzy left her line and went to Kate's side. They kissed briefly. Then their eyes lingered for a moment on each other. Lizzy resisted the urge to touch Kate's cheek. Instead, she smiled tightly. "Hi."

"Hi."

The two women continued to gaze at each other.

"It's Tuesday night," Kate said.

"I was thinking the same thing." Now Lizzy glanced around, breaking their connection and smiling at nothing. Then her eyes came back to rest on Kate. She looked slightly smaller somehow, yet still resolute. "I'm glad to see you," Lizzy added.

"Me, too." There was an awkward pause, then both women started talking at once.

"Did you..."

"I was..."

They both stopped and smiled. "After you," Lizzy said.

"Oh, I was just wondering how you were getting on."

Lizzy nodded, not wanting to be a heavy. "I'm fine. Great! It's been a busy week, you know," she added a little helplessly. Of course, Kate couldn't know because Kate hadn't been with her. She hadn't even shown up at the garage. "How about you?"

"Fine," Kate said. "Everything's fine. Apartment's quite nice. Perfectly comfortable. I'm utterly fine."

"Good."

Lizzy stuck her hands in her pockets. "You still want to go out on Friday?"

They hadn't actually seen each other since the previous Sunday morning when Kate had moved out. Their pending date had loomed large in Lizzy's mind ever since.

Kate nodded. "I do." There was a softening on her face now, and reaching out, she entwined her fingers with Lizzy's. "I'm happy to see you," she said.

Leaning forward, Lizzy gave her a soft kiss. Then a longer kiss.

"Excuse me. Is this your basket?" someone called from the line Lizzy had been in.

Pulling back, Lizzy smiled, reddening. "Yeah, sorry," she called over her shoulder. Then she turned back to Kate. "I'll see you in a few days."

Hope was back, she thought to herself as she took up her place in line once more. Glancing over her shoulder as she unloaded her groceries a moment later, Lizzy caught Kate's eye, and she smiled. Kate nodded and gave her a wave. Then she blew her a kiss.

Turning to pay the cashier, Lizzy felt a streak of jubilation move through her.

There really was hope after all.

*

Where to put the soup?

Holding the can of Ginger Carrot in her hand, Kate opened a kitchen cupboard and searched its half-empty shelves for nothing. It had been exactly four days since she'd moved in, and the vast dark reaches of the cupboards seemed to go on forever. Kate doubted she would ever fill them up.

She spent a few moments putting away her groceries and neatly folding up the paper shopping bag, which she stowed under the sink for lack of a better place. Then once more, she opened the cupboards and stared bleakly. These were just too big. Too empty.

There was no denying it. She missed Lizzy.

She missed their life together. She missed arguing over whether to get the unsliced bread or the sliced bread. She missed falling asleep together, the gentle weight of Lizzy's body pressing into her own. She missed listening to her steady breath in the night. She missed making love on the couch, and in the bed, and in the shower, and wherever they damn well pleased.

She missed talking in the dark in the morning before either of them was fully awake or even coherent. Yet there they were, still holding on to each other for dear life.

These empty cupboards would never be full enough. The single can of soup sitting nakedly beside the small bottles of extra virgin olive oil and balsamic vinegar and the lone box of cereal would forever rebuke Kate for her mistake. As would the spice cupboard containing only salt, pepper, and a small orange box of baking soda. The refrigerator with its gleaming cream interior and too tidy glass shelves looked even more vacant.

There was nothing to be done. She was alone now. Kate had gotten exactly what she thought she wanted.

All that was missing was the peace and happiness.

*

Delilah sat bolt upright. She was sweating profusely.

In her dream, an MRI machine had just broken down and refused to release her body. "Let me out of here!" she kept yelling, but no attendant came.

Tenika snapped on the light.

"What's going on?" she asked. Tenika propped herself up on an elbow and yawned. She looked at the clock. "We've still got three more hours."

"I know. I know. I'm sorry. I…," Delilah couldn't finish her sentence for the fact was she was scared. Very scared. She looked at the ceiling and sighed. "I think I'm claustrophobic."

Tenika put a lazy hand on her back. "Come here," she said.

Delilah snuggled once again in her partner's arms. "I don't know if I can do this."

"You can do this, honey. Millions of people have had MRIs. Don't forget that."

"I know, but what if my dream was prophetic? What if just this one time...." Tenika shushed her and snapped off the light.

"Come on now, baby. This isn't going to help you."

"You're right." Tenika was always right. That was the maddening, incredible, and ultimately lovable thing about her partner. She always knew the deal. "Okay, I won't go there."

Tenika kissed her forehead now. "That's all it takes," she said. "Just breathe and relax. I'll be right there in the room with you, and I'm not going to let anything happen. You're going to be fine."

Delilah could feel her heartbeat slowing. Her breath was becoming even again. "Okay," she agreed. Yawning, she closed her eyes again. "Good."

"Everything's going to be fine."

Slowly the two women began to move, once again, towards sleep. And once again, Delilah thanked the gods for this woman beside her.

Her rock. Her love.

Chapter Fifteen

Delilah lay down on the sliding bed of the MRI machine, clutched her hospital gown to her freezing cold body, and looked up at the attendant nervously. Two feet behind her head, the massive round plastic orifice lay open and waiting for her. She'd already surrendered her clothing, her earrings, and her tiny nose ring. She took one breath and then another.

She felt utterly naked and afraid.

The attendant, a woman in black scrubs with spiky gray hair, did her best to be reassuring, but Delilah wasn't buying it. The nightmare from the night before was still seared into her brain.

"You'll be fine. It will be over in no time," soothed the attendant as she lowered a small plastic cage over Delilah's head. Nimbly she stuffed two small pillows into position over Delilah's ears. "That's for the noise," she explained. "Gets a little loud in there." The effect was like wearing a muffled version of a goalkeeper's mask.

Great, Delilah thought grimly. Gazing into the small mirror installed overhead, she scanned her immediate surroundings for Tenika. At that exact moment, Tenika intuitively reached over and squeezed her hand. As her fingers closed around Delilah's, some small measure of relief eased through her body.

"Okay, we're all set," the technician said. "I'll be right here making sure you're fine. And your friend…," The woman hesitated. "Partner," corrected Tenika.

"Your partner will be just on the other side of the glass, too," she carried on smoothly, the voice of comfort. "So are you ready?"

Delilah took a deep breath and closed her eyes. "Ready." She wasn't, of course, but that was academic. She was doing this whether she liked it or not.

The technician worked the controls, and Delilah slid inside the machine, releasing Tenika's fingers as she went. The huge plastic machine felt like a high-tech sarcophagus as it engulfed her. Only a few inches separated the head gear that surrounded her brain from the impenetrable wall of the machine. It felt like a place with no escape. Her heart began pounding inside her chest.

Delilah heard the door shut as the technician and Tenika left the room. She had been left alone in the MRI scanner. Immediately, she wondered how quickly she could get out of there.

She took one breath, then two, trying to calm herself as the machine began its work. Making several loud bangs and clunks, the magnetic camera swung into action. A blaring blast of sound surrounded her as the camera began to shoot. It was a cross between a jackhammer and a severe warning alarm, the sort used on a factory assembly line when someone was about to lose an arm or a leg. Every few seconds or so, the racket would blast through her skull, moving easily past the ear pillows.

Delilah felt extremely small. Closing her eyes, she did her best to lay still as the noises surrounding her continued, unabated. Shakily, Delilah kept taking deep breaths, trying to ease the panic that was building in her body.

"How ya doin'?" The technician's chipper voice crackled through the intercom.

"Fine," Delilah lied. But she wasn't fine, of course. She was more stressed out than ever. She broke into a sweat as she lay there, motionless. All she wanted was for the MRI to end, the doctor to give his opinion, and the question of her tremor to finally be answered. Closing her eyes, Delilah began to count back from 100 to zero.

Long minutes stretched by. Then finally, the camera and its attendant cacophony stopped. Everything was silent until the technician reappeared a moment later. Shakily, Delilah swallowed, unsure if the ordeal was over. A moment later, she came sliding out of the machine. "Wasn't so bad, right?" the technician asked.

Delilah just looked at her.

Tenika appeared in the doorway and their eyes met. "Hey," she called. "You alright?"

All Delilah could do was nod. With every fiber of her being, she wanted to be out of there, and somehow Tenika knew this, too. Sweeping her out of the room, Tenika's arm came around her, hustling her back towards the dressing room and her clothing. "Good work," Tenika whispered in her ear. "You got it done."

Delilah wiped away the tears in her eyes. "Yeah."

She just wanted to go home.

*

"Let's begin by getting to know each other," the therapist suggested. The small mousy woman with the big tortoiseshell glasses looked at Frankie encouragingly. "Why don't you tell me what brought you here today?"

Frankie sat back and glanced around. Nervously her fingers beat a tattoo on her thigh. "Well, you know, I have some stress. I'm a police officer. I think I mentioned that in my voicemail."

"Yes. Go on."

Frankie paused. Then she looked more critically at her new potential therapist. "Wait. Shouldn't I be asking the questions?" she said. After all, Frankie reasoned, she was the one who was shopping.

The therapist seemed slightly taken aback. "Oh. Well, what question would you like to ask?"

"Questions, doc. Questions, plural. If we're going to do this thing, I need to know more about you. I mean, I read your profile online. You've got the degrees and everything. But I know nothing about how you work, or anything, really."

The therapist put down her notepad and regarded Frankie. "Go on."

"Well, for instance. I'd like to know your sexuality. How do you identify yourself?"

The therapist gave a small prim smile. "I don't generally discuss these matters with clients."

Frankie sniffed. Just like she thought. "So you're not saying then?"

Now the therapist gave a broader smile. "No," she said beatifically. "I don't think it's germane."

It's germane if I'm frigging asking it, Frankie thought to herself. But then, she knew it would be like this.

"Have you ever worked with a police officer before?" Frankie pressed.

"I've worked with a broad variety of clients," the therapist said. "But…"

"Well, no police officers per se, but…"

"So the answer is 'no,' correct?"

The therapist's beatific smile was gone now. Instead, she studied the notebook in her lap. Looking up, she posed a question to Frankie. "Are you carrying a weapon right now?"

Now this. Jesus.

"Doc, I always carry a weapon. It's part of my job. In some states, it's mandated that we're always armed."

The therapist leaned forward in her seat and began speaking to Frankie in a low, intense voice. "I want you to take out your gun, and put it on my desk over there. Then we can continue. And you are never permitted to carry a weapon in here again."

Frankie stood up. But she didn't remove her gun. Instead she put her hands on her hips. "I think we're done here," she announced.

The therapist looked at her in wonder and said nothing.

"I could have told you it was going to go like this," Frankie said, moving towards the door. "Thanks anyway."

"But wait..." the therapist called out as Frankie shut her office door.

Taking the steps to the street two at a time, Frankie got out of there as fast as she could. It would be a cold day in hell before she'd lay it all down for some shrink who didn't understand the first basic thing about her life.

And no, she wouldn't be removing her weapon anytime soon. *How freaking arbitrary was that?*

When she got to the bottom of the stairs, Frankie turned up the street and began to walk in big furious strides. She had the rest of her day off to kill, but really, right now, there was only one place she wanted to go. She needed to calm down. To get a little perspective.

She was heading back to Driven.

*

"Check this out." Tenika's voice was emphatic. "I swear that's Kate right there behind her in the picture. Look."

Tenika handed a small stack of black and white photocopies over to Lizzy. She peered at the top sheet curiously. "Where'd you get these?" Lizzy asked.

"That one's *US Weekly*. Mindy Rose is all over that rag. I found them in the library. I got copies from *People, Woman's World*, the usual tabloids. Everywhere Mindy went, Kate went too, right?" She turned to another page in the stack. "Look here. That's definitely Kate in the baseball cap, isn't it? Way over on the side?"

Lizzy nodded. "It totally is." She glanced up at her business partner. "Nice work. Think these would hold up as evidence?"

Across the garage, Frankie looked up from the conversation

corner where she was currently the only customer. Clearly she was listening to their conversation.

"I assume so. I mean, I don't know for sure…." Tenika's voice fell away for a moment. "Someone's got to believe us."

"Kate's bound to have emails, receipts, photographs of her own. That kind of thing," Tenika continued.

"But then I'd have to tell her that Mindy's been threatening us."

Frankie stood up now and began advancing rapidly on the two women. "Excuse me," she said as she neared them. "I don't want to intrude, but did you just say someone's been threatening you?"

Tenika and Lizzy looked at each other. "No, it's okay, Frankie. It's no big deal," Lizzy said.

Frankie raised her eyebrows. "Threats aren't a small deal."

"No, we've got this is all I'm…," Lizzy started, but Tenika silenced her with a hand on her arm.

"Why do you mention it?" she asked Frankie.

"I don't like to hear that my friends are getting bothered by someone."

"And?" Tenika asked.

Frankie took a breath and folded her arms. "And…okay, I'm a police officer. Maybe I can help."

Lizzy and Tenika looked at each other again. "Didn't know that," Tenika said quietly.

Frankie held up her hands. "Look, I know. I know! The SFPD is under all kinds of scrutiny and there are a lot of bad cops out there, but I swear I'm one of the good ones. I would nev…"

"Frankie, just tell me what you can do for us," Tenika interrupted. She was looking Frankie squarely in the eye.

"Well, for one thing, making threats is a crime. Legally, it's called intimidation. What kind of threats are you receiving, exactly?"

"Someone is threatening to get us closed down. Actually, she's been trying to for a while now," Lizzie said. "It's Kate's former boss. She's mad that Kate quit and came to work for us. But unfortunately, Kate's an undocumented worker. So this person says she's going to turn us in to ICE."

"No physical threats? Stalking? Threats of violence?"

"Not yet at least."

"You haven't dated this person, have you?" Frankie asked.

"God no!" Lizzy sputtered.

Frankie continued her questions. "And you're not related to her, right?" The two women shook their heads.

"Could be classified a hate crime then," Frankie continued, thinking aloud. "She's threatening your property by trying to get the garage closed down, and that's clearly illegal." She turned back to the women. "Does she have a thing against lesbians?"

"Doubt it. She's one, too."

"Could be a hate crime based on race, then."

Tenika nodded. "Good. Let's use it."

"Can you remember exactly what she said when she threatened you?" Frankie asked Lizzy.

Lizzy nodded. "Yeah. Tenika was there, too. We can reconstruct it."

"No other witnesses?"

"I don't think so," said Tenika.

"We were here alone," Lizzy agreed.

"That's enough. People really can't go around threatening to take you out of business," Frankie said. "Go file a report with the OPD. They'll tell you what to do next. Sounds like a simple civil harassment case to me. You should be able to shut her down with a temporary restraining order."

Tenika and Lizzy glanced at each other. "How long do they last?" Tenika asked.

"Depends. A full restraining order can be as long as five years. Usually they give you three to start."

For the first time all day, Tenika smiled. *"Now* we're talking."

"Yeah, but wait a minute," Lizzy began.

"Come on, Lizzy, let's do this thing!" Tenika urged, but Lizzy shook her head.

"It's that whole you-go-low, we-go-high thing, T. I get why you're suggesting this, Frankie, and I totally appreciate it. But a restraining order is a big deal."

Tenika threw up her hands. "Lizzy, our business is at stake here. That's a big deal, too!"

"Or not," Lizzy pressed. "I mean, I just don't want to stoop to her level. Anyway, maybe she was just bluffing. And we don't have a lawyer or the money for one, T. Who knows if you can even do this sort of thing yourself?"

"Well, you can," Frankie said. "There's a self-help center out at the Hayward courthouse. You have to be able to show the judge some evidence to back up your case. You'd have a bunch of different things, ideally. But basically, it's pretty simple. You can do it all yourself, except for serving the papers. A friend can do that part. Once you get the summons served, you file the papers and show up for the hearing in front of a judge." Frankie paused. "It sounds to me like you've got a case. If she actually did threaten your business."

"Oh, she did all right," Tenika muttered. "Numerous times."

Lizzy sighed and shifted uncomfortably. "Let me think about it. It just seems like…a big move, you know what I'm saying?"

The other two looked at her, not comprehending, and Lizzy held up her hand. "Just give me time," she said. "I'll think about it."

"Up to you," Tenika said, eyebrows raised. "Until it's not." She turned to Frankie and extended her hand. "And thanks, Frankie. That was good of you." The two women shook hands.

"Call me for help," Frankie said. "I'll do whatever I can."

Lizzy turned back to the rear tire she was replacing as Frankie returned to her couch in the conversation corner. Could defusing Mindy Rose really be that simple?

Somehow Lizzy doubted it.

*

Sally and Lizzy meandered through the quiet walkways of the Morcom Rose Garden. The bushes were at peak, and the garden was overflowing with blooms.

Carefully cultivated roses of every size, color, and shade imaginable sprang forth around them as they walked the paths. Some cascaded into virtual walls of white, cerise, and pink blossoms. Others were organized in beds, hybrid cultivar beauties in subtle shades of lavender, deep burgundy, peach and wild stripes of crimson and white.

But even so, the place was oddly vacant. The Morcom Rose Garden was a long-forgotten Oakland treasure, a remnant of times gone by.

Sally and Lizzy still had at least an hour of sunlight left as they headed up a path in the center of the garden. The stone pathway was flanked by cultivated rose trees in shades of yellow and peach, and slightly weedy beds that had seen better times. The path before them was festooned with small brass plaques bearing the names of various women. A nearby sign designated it "The Mother of The Year Walkway."

"Thanks again for meeting up with me," Lizzy said. She felt a little shy with Sally, for the fact was she barely knew her.

"My pleasure," Sally replied. She smiled easily at Lizzy. "Tenika said you're dealing with some heavy things."

Lizzy looked askance. She never wanted to be the one in the room with problems. "Okay, well, yeah. I guess so," she finally said. How was she supposed to get into this? "But first, tell me about you," she countered.

"I'm happy," Sally said simply.

"And?"

"That's kind of my whole story." Sally glanced over at Lizzy. She did, indeed, seem genuinely content. "Why do you ask?"

Lizzy gave up. She shook her head in chagrin. "I don't know,

Sally. I guess I just feel funny spilling all my problems to you. It feels like a whole lot of drama, you know?"

Sally shrugged. "I'm here to help. If I can."

"You're incredibly kind. Thank you." Lizzy took an uneasy breath. "The fact is that T told me to talk to you, so here I am."

"Go on. I'm listening."

"She said you read cards, and people's future, and stuff…" Lizzy's voice trailed away.

"I do, more or less thinking. I'm thinking lawyers are hella expensive."

Lizzy stuck her hands in her pockets as they slowly walked on. "I don't know, Sally. I'm just kind of going nuts here. Any kind of advice would help." They stopped by an especially abundant white rose bower. A young couple was posing for photographs beneath the flowers, while a professional photographer posed them this way and that.

The women discreetly turned away, giving them some space. Then Lizzy stopped and turned to Sally. "The problem is I'm in love with a woman who just moved out. We were living together because we had to, temporarily. It's not over, exactly. We still love each other, but she says she needs to live alone. And the thing is…I thought she was committed." Lizzy's voice trailed off helplessly.

"She *is* still committed," Sally said. Her eyes were focused on the path before them.

Lizzy regarded her curiously. "How do you know?"

She just shrugged.

"Wait! You don't actually know Kate, do you?"

"Kate and I have never met, but I can see who she is. And she loves you, Lizzy. She really does. She needs to know, however, that you love her."

"That I love her! Well, Jesus!" Lizzy threw up her hands in frustration. Then she studied her friend. "With all due respect, Sally, that's where you're wrong. I've told her a million times how much I love her."

Sally shook her head. "That's not what I'm talking about, Lizzy. I'm talking about the commitment that comes with really seeing someone. Seeing them for who they are. Not projecting like crazy to suit your own agenda." She paused. "We all live in illusion, you know," Sally added more gently.

Lizzy's stomach tightened. Sally's words landed like a hard rock in her belly. Yet, there was something to what she was saying, and Lizzy knew it. "Go on," Lizzy said in a small voice.

"You're a romantic. At least that's what I see."

How the hell did she know all of this? "Did T put you up to this?" Lizzy asked, and Sally laughed.

"Believe me, Tenika made a point of *not* telling me anything at all."

Sally had Lizzy's full attention now. "Go on."

"Romantics are people who live in fantasy and illusion. They think love is nothing but sunny skies and rose-filled gardens." Sally looked at Lizzy pointedly. "But they forget about the thorns, and the fungus, and the aphids, and the fact that all these roses are one step closer to death every day. Chances are your Kate is wanting something more than just your proverbial sea of roses, Lizzy."

Lizzy paused and swallowed. "She said she moved out so she could claim her own space," she added quietly.

"And you were hurt."

"Well…yeah."

"That is thinking like a romantic with a single narrow view of how love should be," Sally said. She turned to Lizzy for emphasis. "Your opportunity now is to leave your past behavior behind and let go of any agenda."

Lizzy swallowed as a tear threatened to roll down her cheek. She felt soundly rebuked, though she knew Sally was exactly right.

Sally continued. "You have the chance to start again, Lizzy. But first, you have to slow down and get to know who Kate really

is. What does she need? What does she love? And most of all...
who is she? You may think you know Kate, but I'd say that you don't.
What's living in her heart and soul, Lizzy? Do you even know?"

The threatened tear now rolled down Lizzy's cheek. "No," she
said quietly, "I guess not."

"If you really find out, then you'll know the truth."

They walked on in silence for a moment. "How do you know
all of this?" Lizzy finally asked, but Sally just smiled.

"I listen," she replied. "Then I say exactly what I hear."

Chapter Sixteen

The doorbell rang.

Lizzy looked up from stringing her guitar. There was no good reason for anyone to be at her door.

For a moment, she continued yanking hard on the top E string, winding it tightly around the tuning peg. Wrapping up the wound string with one deft final pull, Lizzy picked up her pliers and neatly clipped the tip.

The doorbell rang again. This time Lizzy put down her guitar and considered answering it. Usually it was Greenpeace. However much she liked those guys, she really didn't have any money for them right now. On the other hand, it could be a neighbor. Even one who needed something.

Lizzy rose and walked to the door.

She opened it to find Mindy Rose standing in front of her, arms crossed, and a look of supreme annoyance on her face. "What's it going to take?" she asked.

Lizzy blinked. "Excuse me?"

Mindy leaned in menacingly. "I said what's it going to take for you to admit that you've broken the law? You're running Driven illegally, Lizzy, and you know it. But like I said, I've already reported you. So it's really just a matter of time until ICE shows up and arrests both of you."

Having delivered her diatribe, Mindy looked at her manicure

and brushed a little imaginary dust from one sharp red fingertip. Then she looked up at Lizzy with a cocksure smile. "Once they do, I get what I want. Which is your business dead, over and finished."

Lizzy tried to close the door, but Mindy quickly blocked it with one pointed black patent leather pump. "Don't walk away," she demanded. "Don't you dare walk away from me. Don't even try, Lizzy. I'm going to bring you down and I'm going to use everything I've got to do..."

But Mindy did not get to finish her sentence because Lizzy had kicked her foot from the door, then slammed and locked the door in her face. Immediately, Mindy began pounding on the door with both fists. She leaned on the doorbell again and again as Lizzy walked back through her apartment to the kitchen.

No matter how far she got from her front door, Lizzy could hear Mindy screaming outside at the top of her lungs. It was hard to hear what she was screaming at first. Finally, Lizzy moved closer to the door, more out of curiosity than anything else. As she drew closer, she could hear Mindy's voice rise into an unbridled all out shriek.

"I AM GOING TO RUIN YOU! YOU ARE ALREADY RUINED! LIZZY!" she screamed. "YOU CANNOT FUCKING HIRE ILLEGALS AND YOU KNOW IT! DRIVEN IS DEAD!"

There was a pause. Then Lizzy heard Mindy shout to any-one listening in the neighborhood. "LIZZY EDGEWOOD IS HIRING ILLEGAL ALIENS...YOUR NEIGHBOR IS BREAKING THE LAW!" There was a pause, and then one single anguished cry.

"DOESN'T ANYONE FUCKING CARE?"

Meanwhile, Lizzy walked back to the kitchen and sank into a chair at her table. She tried to still the pounding of her heart as she considered calling the police. Finally, she decided against it. Mindy would probably leave in another moment.

Sure enough, there was silence from the front now. After another moment, Lizzy peered through the curtains by the door. Mindy and her shiny pink BMW were gone. A neighbor was watering his lawn in the twilight.

Something definitely had to be done.

*

Lizzy cradled the phone as she opened a beer. "I just had Mindy at my front door, losing her shit," she told Tenika.

"No WAY!"

"Way. Anyway, I'm in. Let's get the restraining order."

"Now you're talking, sister." Tenika sounded fairly jubilant on the phone. "We can't have this kind of craziness going on. Not if we have a business to run."

"Yep. I just needed to see her lose it to get how unstable she truly is." Lizzy sighed. "Poor Kate. She put up with that insanity for seven years."

"I can only imagine." Tenika empathized. "Anyway, I've been thinking. Lawyers are hella expensive, so I say we do it ourselves."

Lizzy smiled. If there was one thing she loved, it was seeing her business partner blast towards yet another challenge. Tenika never doubted for one single minute that she could do anything she set her mind to. Pretty much ever.

Now Lizzy spoke up. "I hate to throw cold water on things, T, but she will probably show up with some big ass lawyer at the hearing. She even said as much when she came by the garage."

"Maybe. But consider this. So far, the woman's been a compulsive liar, so she may not show at the hearing at all."

This was true enough.

"Either way," Tenika continued, "we have to get a restraining order on her. This is happening. But listen...Lizzy?"

Lizzy could hear a warning in Tenika's voice. "Uh oh. What?"

"You've got to tell Kate. Like hella."

Lizzy stood up and began to pace the kitchen. "No way! No possible way. Tenika, I am *not* telling Kate." She took a long pull of her beer.

"Lizzy, you have to, and here's why. For one thing, this is about her. She deserves to know what's happening, right? And she will be able to help us here. Nobody knows Mindy better than Kate."

Lizzy looked out the window at a squirrel running through a neighboring tree. "It's not happening, T. No way in hell."

"Can I just ask why?"

Lizzy sighed. "Because Kate is alone, that's why. We've barely seen each other. She has enough to worry about without this on her mind, too."

"Well, that's very sensitive and caring and everything, Lizzy, but get a grip, girl. You've got to tell her. We need Kate."

"T, please. It's only a hearing for a restraining order. How hard can it be? It's not like…a trial, right?"

Both of them stopped for a moment of shared, uncertain silence. "Are you sure?" Tenika asked.

"Yeah." Lizzy paused. In truth, she had no idea. "I mean, I think so. That's what Frankie said, at least. It's just a hearing with a judge, right? We just fill out some forms." She paused again and tried to keep the pleading out of her voice. "Please, T. Don't make me tell Kate. It's…delicate, right now."

There was a pause. "Okay," Tenika finally said. "But I don't like all this secret stuff. It's not healthy."

"I'm asking you. As a friend."

Tenika sighed. "I get it. I don't like it. But I get it."

A moment later, they hung up, and Lizzy sat there for a moment with their decision. They would take Mindy on. And as for Kate, she'd find out eventually, when the time was right.

For now, Lizzy had to bend over backwards not to be too clingy or in any way needy. In the end, it was all about protecting Kate.

*

"Damn!" Tenika peered at the computer screen. "This is going to cost us almost $400."

She was sitting in front of the laptop in her underwear, unable to tear herself away. Behind her, Delilah lounged on the bed, reading and moving towards sleep. She looked up. "Sounds pricey."

"I hate this shit." Tenika looked up in annoyance. "We can't even get a fee waiver. You have to be on food stamps or something." She got up and strode towards the bed. "I'm annoyed I have to deal with Mindy Rose at all. And then to have to pay for it!" Tenika sat down wearily on the bed and looked at her partner. "What did we do to deserve this?"

Delilah didn't look up from her book. "People like her can't stand people like you. Especially if you're in her way."

"Yeah, well, we are definitely getting someone else to serve the summons." She looked at her partner. "I was thinking maybe Sally could do it. I mean, I'd ask you, but you have a lot on right now."

Delilah put down her book. "Oh, honey, I'd do it," she said, "if you wanted me to."

"I'm not saying Sally owes us a favor, but ..."

"She owes us a favor," Delilah affirmed. "If you want, I'll go with her. We can do it together."

Tenika smiled at her partner. "I appreciate you, baby, but Sally can cover it," she said. Then leaning over, she kissed her gently.

"Come here, you," Delilah said, pulling her partner closer. Now Tenika lowered herself over Delilah's waiting body and ran a hand down her beautiful alabaster thigh. Once again, she began the slow tender dance that always preceded their lovemaking.

Bodies connected, parts intertwined, heat built as they moved together across the bed. In another moment, Delilah was orgasming silently, holding on to the headboard for dear life and doing her best not to disturb their friend, asleep in the next room. Their friend who would soon serve Mindy Rose a summons.

Tenika's fingers entered her again and again, and she surrendered to the complete and total rightness of their deep connection. Once again, she understood perfectly. This was what she'd shown up for. This was their love, however it was meant to be. Messy, raw, and perfect, in no uncertain terms.

A few moments later, as she lay in Tenika's arms, Delilah once again felt the wave of deep gratitude for their life together. Somehow, her rock-solid need to get married was lifting, just the slightest bit.

Delilah knew it. She was right where she belonged.

*

Just across 580, deep in the Laurel, Kate was making plans. She'd just texted Lizzy and invited her to come over for dinner on Saturday night.

It was time to be in touch. Other than bumping into each other at Berkeley Bowl earlier in the week, their contact had been scarce. Lizzy hadn't called and texted copiously. Instead, she'd done what Kate really needed, which was to give her plenty of space. In fact, she'd barely texted or called Kate at all, despite her promises to when she left.

Kate checked her phone again. Lizzy hadn't even responded to Kate's invitation yet, and it had been nearly an hour. She was sure Lizzy was deep into some project or other at this moment. Idly, she wondered what that could be.

It wasn't Lizzy's rehearsal night. Nor was it likely that she'd stepped out to a movie or a show. Lizzy regarded weeknights as school nights, and usually she had a strict early-to-bed policy.

Unless, somehow in her semi-but-not-really-single status, she'd decided to step out and hit one of the lesbian-friendly bars in San Francisco.

Kate shook off her thoughts and focused on what to serve for dinner the following night. Lizzy loved her Irish stew—that had been established. But if she actually put aside the time to make it, would it be perceived as a nostalgic nod to the small family rituals that had made up their life when they lived together? Sunday was always Irish stew night.

And if it did, was she ready for that? After all, Kate had been living on her own for less than one week. She took a deep breath and got up from the couch where she'd been flipping through recipes on social media.

Kate began to pace through the apartment. She needed to be measured and in control when she saw Lizzy. She couldn't just abandon herself to her loneliness. Because the fact was, she missed her lover terribly.

Kate pulled her phone out of her pocket and glanced at it once more. Still, nothing.

Lizzy wasn't getting back to her. *Come now, you've been here before*, Kate chided herself.

She'd been alone for the better part of eight years, pretty much the entire time she'd lived in the U.S. Kate was so used to being single that it had become kind of a petrified state of being for her. The fact that Lizzy swept in and split that endless petrification right in two was still stunning to her.

What, exactly, had happened?

Lizzy had happened, pure and simple. Her presence—her eyes, her warmth, her strength, and her incredible ability to tune into Kate and read her perfectly—elevated her far above the half dozen women Kate had dutifully gone out with on one or two wan dates. And then once they began to make love…well, Kate had simply surrendered at that point.

Lizzy had been like a tornado in her midst, a force field Kate was incapable of resisting. Even just to glance at Lizzy's naked body, as she came upon her in the apartment, produced a silent but reliable thrill every time. Lizzy was bigger than life. And Lizzy was all hers.

Or at least she hoped she still was.

One more time, Kate pulled her phone out of her pocket. Still no reply. *To hell with it*, she thought, as she flipped over to her favorites list and touched Lizzy's name. She was calling her.

She had to.

Still, Lizzy's voicemail clicked on. Kate left no message and hung up, slightly bewildered. *Where in God's name was she?*

It was, of course, possible something had happened. Perhaps Lizzy had gotten sideswiped on her bike. Silently, Kate cursed the bloody bike that she insisted on riding every damn night to hell and back. On the street. In Oakland. With trucks going by only inches away.

Kate just hoped that this time she had her helmet. God forbid Lizzy had discovered the electric scooters now whizzing this way and that, carrying their un-helmeted occupants within an inch of death as they rode in the street, carefree.

Kate closed her eyes and sent up a prayer to whatever force might actually happen to be listening.

Please take care of Lizzy. My Lizzy. Wherever she is and whatever she is doing.

Then once again turning to social media, she began to construct the perfect romantic dinner for two.

Chapter Seventeen

The early morning spin class at the Y was usually the place Tenika could lay down her troubles. But today, they seemed to be keeping pace with her wildly spinning stationary bike. Darren, the instructor, was pounding out his usual curated R&B selections.

Today's musical anchor was something he called "the Philly sound." MFSBs theme song to Soul Train cranked through the studio as a dozen fellow members hunkered down, pumping fast in their own personal orange zone. Darren was a black, sixty-something music head who had found his way into the perfect blend of intense spin instruction and upbeat music curation.

"Uno, dos, tres, *quatro!*" he exhorted. Twelve spinners all stood up in tandem on the count of four and began pushing ever harder.

Darren's head beat in perfect rhythm with the now soaring strings and pounding rhythm track. "This is MFSB...Mothers, Fathers, Sisters, Brothers. The house band for Philadelphia International Records. *Hnnh!*" he exulted as he got his own groove going on his bike. "Catch that *beat!*"

Halfway into the class, Tenika was now pouring sweat. This was why she came here, to get the endorphins rolling to the point that life became a totally pain-free blur of bliss. She showed up every week without fail, simply because she had to. It felt that good. And now she needed that release more than ever.

For one thing, it had been two days since Delilah's MRI, and they still had no answer. The doctor told them it would take a little time. "A day or so," were his exact words, but it had now been 48 hours. Not having any experience with this, Tenika could only imagine that no news was very bad news indeed.

Perhaps the doctor was calling Delilah right now, gravely asking her to come in to discuss the results. Perhaps by the end of the day, they'd both be reading up on brain tumor surgery and treatment options. Perhaps Delilah had an aggressive cancer that would sweep through her body and basically kill her within a few months.

Such things had most definitely happened.

Once again, Tenika reminded herself that she had no freaking idea what the deal was. None at all. There could be nothing. Or there could be something. And until they knew something, they most certainly would not know anything at all.

Then there was the matter of getting a restraining order against Mindy Rose. This Tenika felt far more confident about. She knew how to fill out forms, stand in line, and recite the facts as well as anyone. How hard could it be? What bothered her was this whole business of not telling Kate about it. But that was Lizzy's business, not hers.

Tenika figured she had her hands full without getting into that little piece of micromanagement.

Still her worry about Delilah slowly burned on. Darren dug into a final, excruciating set of high intensity intervals. Tenika closed her eyes, feeling the music fill the space around her, as her body surrendered to the red zone. This is what she came for, she reminded herself, as she turned the small red knob on the bike to the right. She was getting it done.

Her sweat poured furiously now, and she wiped her face on the gym towel that was draped over the handlebars of her bike. Pushing along against that higher pressure, a sudden unexpected thought popped into her head.

Just marry her.

Tenika closed her eyes against the hard effort the bike required, and panting, pushed on. The thought repeated itself a third time.

Just marry her.

Now she opened her eyes and looked around. Tenika wasn't given to receiving messages and certainly not ones that urged her to marry someone. Still. The message lingered.

Just marry her.

Where the hell was this coming from?

Of course, Tenika didn't even need to ask because she knew perfectly well where this was coming from. It was coming from that unknowable place deep inside of her where the most honest answers always lay. If she'd actually been wondering about marrying Delilah. Which she hadn't.

Or had she?

Tenika put her head down and pushed her way through the final red zone interval. Then cranking her little red knob to the left, she took all the pressure off the bike, and sitting back on her saddle, began to cycle slowly. Meditatively.

Now Teddy Pendergrass's voice filled the studio as he crooned his way into *Love TKO.* As if on cue, the instructor spoke up. "I've been married 40 years," he said, "That was a total love TKO. Wasn't my only one, y'all. But it was the big one."

The big one. *Was Delilah the big one?*

Teddy was now singing about letting love control him, about having a total change of mind. And as his liquid chocolate voice filled the room, Tenika thought about Delilah in her hospital gown sliding inside the MRI machine. And how she had hung on to Tenika's fingers until the last possible moment. How vulnerable she'd seemed, with only her bare feet and her legs protruding from the machine that was scanning her head in inscrutable detail for a life-threatening disease.

She thought about making love with Delilah only the night before, and how willing Delilah had been to jump in and help Tenika with the hearing.

Tenika closed her eyes as one tear and then another sprang into her eyes. Then she recoiled. She did not want to cry, right here in the middle of Deep Soul Cycle. No way in hell. But she could no longer deny what was going on.

"Bring your pedals to a gentle conclusion," said Darren. "And when you're ready, stand up on the bike for a brief balancing act, touching your fingertips to the handlebars."

Tenika stood and balanced, and as she did, she knew what she had to do.

She needed to marry Delilah.

*

Frankie felt naked, and she didn't like it. Not one bit.

This time the therapist was a pretty blonde with a captivating smile. Her manner was warm and genuine. "I've worked with all kinds of people," she said to Frankie's now usual first question. "Law enforcement included."

"I mean...I've seen stuff. Really bad stuff," Frankie said.

"I'm sure you have," the therapist replied. "EMDR has been proven effective again and again with these types of trauma."

There was a pause. Then the therapist continued, "Not that it's a foregone conclusion that you have PTSD."

"I do," Frankie said. "I mean, I think I do. Tell me what this is, okay? Nightmares. Instant replays. I'm as jumpy as a cat. I can't stand to live in my own body half the time."

"You're referring to something specific that happened while you were on duty?"

"Yeah," Frankie said, her voice growing gruff. Just the mere mention of it was unsettling. She closed her eyes against the sudden intrusion of these thoughts.

The therapist was listening intently. "Let's start there," she said.

Frankie's eyes widened slightly. "Right...now?"

"Sure. See if you can pinpoint a specific, troubling memory. That is how we begin the EMDR process."

Frankie eyed her uncertainly for a moment, but she also knew that at some level her die had been cast. She could go on evaluating therapists forever, or she could just start to resolve the problem. "Maybe," she said, "but how long is this going to take?"

The therapist glanced down at the notebook in her lap. "Sixty minutes. Maybe less."

"No, I mean, will this take years of therapy?"

The therapist smiled. "No, Frankie. Most first responders need about five or six sessions."

"That's it? For everything?"

"That's it. I work with these." The therapist picked up a pair of gray plastic pods and a control box from the small table between them. She handed the pods over to Frankie.

"You put one in each hand, and they vibrate in sequence, right and left. They create the bilateral stimulation in the brain that helps it to reprogram."

The pretty blonde leaned forward "Why don't we just try some EMDR right now? If you're willing."

What the hell? Frankie suddenly felt utterly resigned. At some point, she was going to have to deal with this, so it might as well be now. "Okay," she heard herself say. She took in a breath and set her jaw. "Let's go."

*

Exactly forty-seven minutes later, Frankie opened her eyes. She was utterly exhausted, and her shirt was soaked in sweat. Yet she had a singular sense of hope.

She looked at the therapist and laughed out loud. "What the hell just happened?"

One moment she'd been sizing up the entire EMDR process. The next she was recounting every last detail of the stab wounds on the girl's abdomen and groin, and her unseeing brown eyes that stared, motionless, in the beam of Frankie's flashlight. And how she'd checked to see if the girl was breathing, not because she believed she was alive, but because protocol insisted she did.

It was obvious this child was dead. What took Frankie by surprise was the intense panic she felt that night as she assessed the crime scene. How repulsed she was by the girl's naked, brutalized body. And how many times it had revisited her in slow-mo, gory detail.

Over the course of the next forty-seven minutes—time that had basically evaporated into nothing—Frankie had been on a ride inside her brain that she now was incapable of comprehending. Of even fully remembering.

She'd been screaming at one point, convinced someone would die. At another, she was no more than four years old, staring into the eyes of her older sister when she was delirious and then unconscious with febrile seizures. Somehow Frankie had ridden one thought after another into a memory she didn't even entirely recognize. Yet, her body did, in amazingly vivid detail. Every last fiber of that experience had been seared into her memory and her consciousness.

Now Frankie wanted more. Especially the part where she rebuilt the memories once the panic, the uncertainty, and the simple pain of being a child in an overwhelming situation had eased.

In her new memory, Frankie had gone to her mother, asked for reassurance that her sister would be all right, and received it.

Her mother's face had been painted with love, and she held Frankie and reassured her. "It will all be okay," she soothed. And now, Frankie knew it would be.

She grinned at the therapist. "Wow."

"You did some excellent work there, Frankie. How do you feel?"

Frankie shook her head. "I mean...wow."

"The body never forgets," the therapist said.

Moments later, Frankie slowly walked out, climbed in her car, and began a slow thoughtful drive back to Oakland from El Cerrito. She was going to get over this thing. She could feel it.

She'd just found the answer to her problems.

*

"Nice suit." Tenika nodded approvingly at Sally as she walked into the garage. The gray pantsuit, along with the dingy gray and blue backpack on her back, gave her the sleek, slightly harried look of a legal aid lawyer. She'd added an ivory blouse and a string of pearls from god knew where.

"You like it?" Sally asked. "Twenty-five bucks at a consignment store in the Fruitvale."

"Where'd you get the pearls?"

"They were my Aunt Helen's. I knew I'd probably need them some day."

"Sweet." Tenika peeled off her purple latex gloves, blackened with engine grease. "Lizzy should be back with the summons any moment." She studied Sally and gave an approving nod. "Seriously. You look very professional."

Sally shrugged. "This is me dressing like an adult. I can't wait to take the damn thing off. And forget these pumps. You ever wear these things?"

Tenika laughed. "Hell no!"

The plan was that Sally would take the summons and court paperwork over to Mindy Rose's garage, and posing as media, try to get a quote. She would deliver the package directly to Mindy in her office.

"I don't think this woman has any idea what's coming," Tenika said. "She's just that clueless, right?"

Sally shrugged. "If you say so."

"Sally!" Lizzy appeared, slightly breathless, and handed over a standard-looking large yellow envelope to Sally.

"That's it?" Tenika asked. "Looks kind of unassuming."

"Yeah, but it packs a punch," Lizzy said. "When it comes to legalese you just can't argue, you know what I'm saying? All those forms are in there, signed, sealed, and stamped. It's got *presence.*"

"Cool." Tenika turned to Sally now. "So you're clear on what to do? And you know what Mindy looks like, right?"

Sally nodded. "Yeah, I've seen her picture. So I just go in there, verify it's her, and give her the documents. She takes them, and I walk out."

"Yeah," Tenika said. "Except that she might not take the forms, right? She might tear them up. She might refuse to accept it or put it in the trash. Hell, she'll probably throw you out of her office while she's at it. But that's okay. You've already served the papers, so it still counts."

"Then you come back here and fill out the Proof of Summons," Lizzy added. "That's like the most important thing."

"Got it," Sally said. She zipped the large envelope into her backpack. "Seems simple enough."

A moment later, Lizzy and Tenika watched Sally head crisply out the door of the garage.

Justice was about to be served.

*

Tenika stood outside the closed up storefront on Solano Avenue and rang the buzzer. Peering through the gloom of the darkened shop, she could see the owner's pug sitting in front of the door, regarding her curiously. Around the dog, nearly every surface was filled with antiques and collectibles of every description.

Old Tiffany lamps hung above antiquated state flags that tumbled over box after box of vintage record albums and postcards. Posters for Jean Harlow and something called the Quiet

Man Revolution Band hung alongside knock off impressionist oils, framed in gold above a big sagging red velvet divan.

A stuffed Gila monster, paw raised, appeared poised to take a swipe at the big Buddha head just next to it. Beside it, an old-fashioned privacy screen adorned with faded flowers was draped with a brilliant red fringed Spanish shawl. Some aging white cotton bloomers were primly hung nearby on a hanger.

Over everything lay a fine film of dust. Someone had been collecting things forever.

A moment later, the owner, a balding older White man with a handlebar mustache and a well-worn gray sweater with elbow patches, appeared.

He unlocked the door. "Tanya?" he asked.

"Tenika. Yeah, hi."

The shopkeeper opened the door.

"Sorry. Come in! Follow me." He smiled at her encouragingly as he led her past the first room to a smaller second room in the back. This one was equally dusty and crammed with even more aging paraphernalia than the first. "I've been having all kinds of fun since you called. Pulled some really nice pieces for you. Here. Take a look."

They paused before an open secretary desk. On it was a small black velvet tray, holding an assortment of vintage rings. The shopkeeper pulled up a carved antique chair. "Have a seat," he said.

Tenika cleared her throat and sat down. Then she took a breath. This was it. She was actually picking out a ring for Delilah.

She hesitated as she looked at the spread of vintage diamond rings before her. Immediately, nothing caught her eye. Instead, they all looked small and complicated, fussy little Victorian jumbles of platinum filigree studded with diamonds. They all looked strangely alike, just as she feared they might. None of them appealed to her.

"Hmm," she said, sitting back.

"Nothing to your liking?"

"Not immediately." Tenika regarded the man. "Here's the thing. This ring is for someone with very unique taste. It's got to have…I don't know…a little humor to it. Or originality. Not too classic vintage. Not like all the rest. You know what I'm saying?"

He lowered his head in thought for a moment. "Hmm. Well, let me…" He paused in thought for a moment. Then he looked up brightly. "I actually think I might have something." The shopkeeper's voice trailed away as he disappeared into yet another room beyond this one.

Tenika could hear him rustling around in the other room. At one point, there was a loud scrape as if furniture was being moved. Then his footsteps returned.

"I found this," the shopkeeper said.

The man placed another ring on the black velvet tray. This one was, indeed, entirely different. It was a platinum band with a small diamond Scottie dog on it. Around its neck was a collar, a tiny stripe of bright green enamel. Tenika smiled and looked at it more closely.

It was perfect.

"1928-1930," he continued. "Maybe American, maybe European. That part's unclear." He observed Tenika inspecting the ring. "Do you happen to have a Scottie?"

Tenika glanced up and smiled again. "No, but that's okay. I've got a girlfriend who's going to love it."

Ten minutes later, she walked out of the store, her fingers holding on to the plush velvet box in her pocket. As she made her way down the street, Tenika felt curiously complete. She had no idea what Delilah would say or do when she presented the ring to her.

She only knew it was right. That it was meant to be. This was the same kind of right as the voice that had whispered in her ear nine hours earlier.

The time had finally come for her to trust the Universe. And Delilah.

And herself.

Chapter Eighteen

"Where'd you say you're from?" The young gay man at the desk looked Sally up and down, appraisingly. His attention fixated on the overly wide lapels of her consignment suit jacket.

"I didn't," Sally replied. "Just tell her it's Sally from *People Magazine*. I was hoping to grab a quick quote from her."

The assistant's manner now completely changed. "Ohhh, oh, oh, you're media. Okay. Fine," he said, vehemently nodding his approval. "Let me just check, and I'll be back in a flash."

Sally looked around at the gleaming garage with its polished concrete floors stained an appealing shade of rose, and the half dozen empty massage chairs that sat by the window, beckoning to customers.

A sushi chef behind the tiny sushi bar caught her eye and gave a small stiff bow. The place seemed deserted. Apparently Tenika and Lizzy didn't actually have that much to worry about.

The assistant reappeared. "Come this way," he said. He held out his hand. "I'm Gregory, and you are?"

"Just call me Sally."

They arrived at Mindy's office door, and Sally could see she was on the phone. She motioned Sally in impatiently. Then she motioned to the chair across from her. Sally took a seat and studied Mindy, mid-conversation. Putting her backpack on the floor, she unzipped it slightly.

"I'm not doing it. No. No, I told you. I'm not." Mindy's voice rose slightly in agitation, and slightly embarrassed, she smiled at Sally. She held up her finger indicating she would be off the phone in just a moment.

Sally settled into her chair and glanced around. Mindy's office had a pink theme to offset the zebra-striped chairs and the glittering gold stripe in the wallpaper. A highly paid decorator had clearly been in charge, and the effect was a studied version of Vegas. A life-sized framed poster of a slightly younger Mindy in her racing suit, helmet in hand, adorned the wall behind her desk.

"Mindy's at the Indy!" it screamed in bold red letters.

Mindy Rose hung up, and standing up, extended her hand. "Welcome, I'm Mindy," she said, smiling warmly.

Sally smiled back, and fishing into her backpack, she stood as well. Leaning forward, she handed over the fat stack of legal documents that had been in the envelope. "And I'm serving you with this summons," she said.

Mindy's expression went from glowing enthusiasm to disturbed shock, followed quickly by outrage. "What? *What the fuck is this?*" Mindy refused to take the papers Sally was offering her. Instead, she knocked them out of Sally's hand onto the floor, and pointed towards the door. "Who sent you here? If it was Lizzy or Kate, I'm going to fucking kill them!"

Sally picked up the envelope and tossed it on her desk. "You've been served," she said simply as she turned and headed for the door.

"Just...get out... GET OUT!" Mindy sputtered, but Sally was already out the door. The packet of papers came whizzing through the office door behind her, fluttering across the hallway floor.

Sally furiously tapped her way back to the garage entrance. She could hear Mindy screaming down the hallway after her.

"You can tell that FUCKING ingrate Kate that SHE HASN'T GOT A DAMN THING ON ME! And neither do those FUCKING ASSHOLES AT DRIVEN!" Mindy's voice ratcheted up even further into an irate piercing scream that filled the entire garage. Gregory now jumped to his feet in alarm as Sally hurried past, unsure exactly where to look.

Meanwhile, the sushi chef looked on in wonder.

A few seconds later, Sally was out on the sidewalk, her mission complete and her heart pounding wildly. Mindy had been served.

Really, it had gone off like a charm.

*

"Success!" Sally announced as she made her way triumphantly into Driven. Tenika looked over from the car chassis she was working on, and Lizzy jumped up from her stool at the counter. Both women immediately began moving in her direction.

"Alright!" Tenika held out her hand, and they shook.

"So? Details please," Lizzy asked.

"It was great. Amazing, actually. You were totally right," Sally said. "She had no idea. None whatsoever."

Tenika exulted, giving Sally a fist bump. *"Damn!* I love that. I *love* that!"

"Great job," Lizzy added.

"Well, I just wish you could have seen her," Sally began. "Mind if I take these off?" Heading for the couch in the conversation corner, she sat down. Then kicking off her shoes, she rubbed her high-heeled, weary feet.

"Details?" Tenika asked.

"She was smiling up a storm, all ready to give *People* an interview and the next thing she knew... Boom! She'd been served. Mindy was so angry she threw the folder on the floor." Sally sat back and gave a small shrug. "I put it back on her desk before I walked out. But then she threw it all over the hallway as I left."

"Sweet!" Lizzy crowed. "Excellent work."

Sally unwound the long strand of pearls from around her neck and took off the jacket. "She says she's going to kill you both, but I wouldn't worry about that," she added.

"Mindy Rose sure as hell isn't touching this garage," Tenika said. "You got the Proof of Service form?" she asked Lizzy. Lizzy disappeared to retrieve the document. "Nice work," Tenika said to Sally. "I would have loved to have seen her face."

"Hey!" Frankie came walking into the garage, and the two women looked up.

"So Frankie, justice has been served. Or at least the summons has," Tenika announced. "To Mindy Rose?"

"Sally here did the Personal Service work."

Frankie looked over at Sally and gave a small smile. "Nice."

Sally shrugged. "All in a day's work."

Frankie looked puzzled. "Wait—is this actually what you do? You're a professional server?"

Sally laughed out loud. "No! God no. I'd never done it before. I was just helping my friends."

Frankie sat down in the armchair by Sally. "Yeah, you don't seem like the type."

She regarded Sally, sitting there barefoot, wearing a simple silk blouse and a pair of semi-stylish charcoal gray dress pants. Gone were the big Namaste earrings and the hippie scarf. There was something newly dignified about her. And yet, she was still undeniably sexy.

Lizzy returned with the form for Sally to sign. "Here," she said, handing over the Proof of Service and a pen. Sitting down at the table, Sally completed the form.

Lizzy stuck her hands in her pockets and regarded Frankie while they waited. "You here for anything in particular, Frankie?"

Frankie leaned back against her chair. "Honestly, I just needed to relax." She glanced over at Sally. "I just like it here," she explained.

Lizzy nodded. "Okay." She rocked back on her heels for a moment, processing this. "As long as you're good."

Frankie gave an easy smile. "Oh, I'm good."

"Cool." Lizzy smiled as she turned away. Here was the conversation corner, being used exactly as it was originally intended. A place for single lesbians to congregate. Maybe have a coffee. Maybe chat, do a puzzle, or just recover from the stress of life. Maybe even develop a little chemistry.

Lizzy smiled to herself. Kate had been completely right.

As usual.

*

Frankie had been trying not to study the back of Sally's blonde head and the way her gray trousers perfectly set off her beautifully curvy hips. Her eyes kept darting this way and that until finally she gave up. She just needed to look at Sally right now.

It was remarkably soothing to her frazzled nerves.

As if on cue, Sally looked up from completing the form, and turning around in her chair, she gazed over at Frankie.

"I'm glad you're here," Sally said. Immediately, Frankie sat up a little straighter.

Sally gazed at Frankie evenly. "And I want to apologize to you again," she continued. "I was so inappropriate the other night and I know I offended..."

"No, no, no," Frankie shook her head, cutting her off. "I just..." She waved her hands a little helplessly, unable to communicate exactly what she wanted to say. Finally, Frankie just stopped.

"A lot has happened since our date," Frankie finally said. One week had somehow given her enormous perspective. Or one week and an extremely intense EMDR session. "I think I'm the one who owes the apology here," she said.

Still turned in her chair, Sally listened quietly. After a pause, Frankie was emboldened.

"I'm really sorry I was so rude." Frankie looked down at her hands. "I shouldn't have closed down like that. The truth is, Sally, all that stuff you said about me? It freaked me out because it was so true. You were entirely right. I have had a lot of trauma," Frankie hesitated, "especially one in particular, which you described. But… well…I'm working on it."

Her eyes met Sally's, and they exchanged a long look. A spark of connection crackled through Frankie's body. "Anyway, you saw right through me," Frankie chuckled. "So I guess I'm not so tough after all."

Sally smiled. "You don't have to be tough with me."

"Yeah, I get that. The thing is, I'm trained to be tough." Frankie hesitated. "I'm a cop," she finally admitted. "I've seen a lot."

Sally regarded her with a look of deep compassion. Then she smiled, and once more Frankie felt something give inside of her. "And I'm a psychic," Sally said. "That's the kind of thing I often pick up."

Frankie shook her head. "Wow. Really?"

"Mmm-hmm."

"Like … professionally?" Frankie asked, and Sally nodded.

Frankie looked on in amazement. "I'm not generally one for psychics and whatnot. On the force, we think when you're dead, your dead, right? But Sally…I've got to say. You are seriously good at what you do."

Modestly, Sally looked down. "I do what I can. But honestly, I guess I'm just like you."

"How do you mean?"

Once more, Sally's eyes met Frankie's. "I just want to help people," she said.

Frankie reached out her hand now, and Sally took it. "Have dinner with me again," Frankie said, her fingers entwined happily with Sally's. Immediately, she loved the warm graceful feel of Sally's hand in her own. "Please. I promise not to be so difficult."

Sally nodded. "I'd love to," she said. Then giving Frankie's hand a squeeze, she released it.

"I really would," Sally said.

Their next step had clearly arrived.

*

Delilah heard the clatter of the mail slot in her front hall. Putting down her library book, she took a deep breath, steeling herself.

All morning she'd been trying to keep herself busy, knowing that any moment her MRI results would arrive. That at any moment some innocuous-looking envelope would slide onto the floor of her front hall, sealing her fate forever.

Was this going to be a short life or a long life? And if it was short, what was she going to regret? What was she going to wish she'd spent more time, or commitment, or focus on?

And what was going to break her heart when it was all over?

By now, Delilah had a pretty good idea. She kept trying not to think about such things, but still they persisted, lingering at the edge of her day like hungry shadows. If her life was about to end, she knew Tenika was the most important thing, whether she wanted to marry her or not.

Her lover was solid, like a golden rock. And she needed her with all her heart, whether she was healthy or sick.

Rising, Delilah did her best to walk to the front door without running. There was no need to run. One way or another, her die had been cast.

A moment later, she stood, examining the pile of mail on the floor. Slowly, she picked it up from the reddish tiles. The letter from the hospital was the third in the stack of junk mail and catalogs.

Shaking, Delilah took one deep breath and then another as she walked to the couch. She tore at the corner of the envelope. Then hooking a finger in its ragged hold, pulled down to rip the rest of the edge open. The letter slid out easily.

Delilah's eyes moved hurriedly across the page, trying to quickly scan for the expected, dreaded words she feared...*malignancy, terminal, cancer, tumor.*

None were there. Instead, only one sentence appeared on the page.

Your recent MRI scan shows no abnormalities of any kind. Please contact your physician for further instructions.

Sitting back against the couch, Delilah let out a massive sigh. Then immediately, she began to sob. A huge racking wave of relief moved through her body, and all she could do in the moment was let it take her. Loudly she cried, sitting there in the silence of her living room, the dust motes hanging in the air all around her.

She was crying with pure gratitude for this life she loved and for the simple gift of life at all.

And she was crying with the awareness of all she had been given, beginning with Tenika.

Rising, Delilah walked back to the kitchen, and rustling around in a drawer, she pulled out a small grocery pad and a pen. Sitting down, she began to write as a poem now unexpectedly filtering through her consciousness.

Thank You, it began.

No matter what you do, or what I do, here's what I know
You are enough
And I am enough
And together, we are far, far more than enough

Delilah wrote for several more moments, inspired. Then finally, she put down her pen and wiped the tears off of her face.

She needed to write this poem, just like she needed to thank her lover. She smiled, thinking about sharing it with Tenika. She wouldn't rush to call her with her happy news. Instead, she would make it a special evening, just for the two of them tonight.

Then she could thank Tenika properly before she shared her news.

Happily, Delilah sat back and grinned at the ceiling as a glow of life affirming joy poured through her body. If there was a God, she was doing a fantastic job this afternoon. That was for damn sure.

All really would be well.

Chapter Nineteen

Lizzy stood outside Kate's apartment building door and felt a quiver of nervousness. Here she was. This could be everything, or it could be nothing.

She punched the button for Kate's apartment, and a moment later, her voice sounded on the intercom. "Yes?"

Just the sound of her voice struck Lizzy. It felt like it had been a month since they had seen each other at Berkeley Bowl, though in reality it had only been four days. She took a deep breath. "It's me," she replied. Immediately, the buzzer sounded, letting her in.

Kate was waiting for her at the top of the stairs in a bright blue dress. She held the apartment door open and beamed a smile down at Lizzy. Lizzy, in turn, took the steps two at a time. Her heart pounded as she made her way up the stairs to Kate.

They kissed briefly. Then they looked at each other. "I've missed you," Kate said.

Lizzy's heart turned over. Taking Kate in her arms, she folded herself around her, encompassing her in a deep, all-embracing hug. She simply didn't want to let go. Finally, Kate pulled away and took her hand.

"Have a drink," she said, leading her inside. "And dinner."

Lizzy followed her through the door and shut it behind them. Golden late-day sunlight filled the apartment. Despite the fact that there was only a couch and a lamp in the living room, Kate looked remarkably settled in. "This is nice," Lizzy said, taking in the space.

Kate glanced around, hands on hips. "It's alright, I suppose," she said. Then she grinned at Lizzy. "Beer?"

Lizzy nodded. She noticed she felt a little tongue-tied.

She sat down on the couch and watched Kate move through her apartment. This was, most definitely, Kate's space. A few framed prints adorned the walls, and a pretty new oriental rug filled in the otherwise echoing living room.

"I still need some furniture," said Kate, sitting down next to Lizzy. "It feels pretty empty to me."

"New apartments always feel empty at first," Lizzy said.

Kate glanced over at her. "Perhaps. But this one feels *really* empty."

"To filling it up," suggested Lizzy, holding up her beer bottle in a toast.

Kate raised her wine glass. "Yes, to filling it up."

They sat in silence for a moment. Lizzy searched briefly for something to talk about. She still hesitated about bringing up the biggest thing on her mind, the impending hearing against Mindy Rose. The last thing she wanted to do was worry Kate. Yet as she thought about it, Sally's words rang true in her head.

Kate did, indeed, need to know.

"Are you getting some new clients?" Lizzy finally asked.

Kate beamed. "Yes. Two already—and maybe a third. I'll know about that one next week."

"Hey! That's really wonderful. I'm glad for you."

"Oh good Lord, I'm relieved. Turns out the immigration status is a non-issue. No one asks, and I don't tell them. They just want results, and I have to say, I have been getting them."

Lizzy gazed over at Kate happily. "Of course you have. You're awesome. Meanwhile, the conversation corner is totally turning into the place to be. We have a few women who just come and hang out there now. They don't even need repairs."

"That's wonderful." Kate seemed genuinely pleased. Then a wistful look came over her face. "I must admit, Lizzy. I do miss Driven."

Lizzy looked at her somberly. "Driven misses you." She swallowed. "So do I."

Kate nodded. "I know." A small wave of sadness passed across her face. "We'll talk," she said. "Later." Kate stood up and held out her hand. "Let's finish making dinner together."

Gratefully, Lizzy took her hand and followed her back to the kitchen. This was just what she'd come for.

Within a moment, they were ensconced in their old routine. Lizzy was peering under pot lids, asking Kate about this and that. Meanwhile, Kate moved easily from fridge to counter to stove, chopping, stirring, and chatting as she went.

Lizzy lifted the largest lid. "Is this what I think it is?"

"Irish stew," Kate said. "I know it's not Sunday night, but..."

Lizzy beamed back at her. It was her favorite. Kate stopped in front of Lizzy and looked up at her with an expression of deep wistful appreciation. "I really have missed you," she said.

"Yeah, me too." The two women gazed at each other. Nothing had changed at all in their week apart, it seemed.

Leaning over, Lizzy kissed her. Then she kissed her again, this time pulling Kate's willing body close to her own. Lizzy pulled back and ran her hand through Kate's hair. "I'm..." Emotion overcame her for a moment. "I'm so glad to see you," she finally said.

Kate nodded and kissed her again, her tongue finding its way into Lizzy's mouth. They kissed and kissed, standing there in the middle of the kitchen, until finally, inevitably, they began a slow wordless walk towards the bedroom, mouths glued together in an endless kiss, strewing clothing as they went.

Soon a trail of shirts, shoes, panties, bras, and one blue dress lined the floor to the bed, as Lizzy and Kate slid, naked, between the sheets. Soon they found their rhythm again. Breath quickening, they moved together, hands exploring, tongues probing. Moving faster and faster, together they surrendered, first to Kate's climax and then to Lizzy's.

Finally, Lizzy sat up. She looked over at Kate in the gathering spring dusk, and she smiled lazily. "Hey...so was that supposed to happen?"

Kate pulled her back down beside her and hooked her leg inside of Lizzy's, so her thigh rubbed against Kate's vulva. "Yes," she said, kissing Lizzy's throat.

"Okay," Lizzy nodded. "Just catching up." She smiled at her partner. "Nice bed," she said, patting the mattress.

"It's alright," Kate shrugged. "It's too big, really."

"I can fix that," Lizzy said.

Kate agreed with a smile. "I'm sure you can."

Lizzy propped herself up on her elbow and took a deep sniff. Then she sat up, slightly alarmed. "Hey, wait! Is there something we're supposed to..."

Suddenly, Kate sat bolt upright. "Oh sweet Jesus! The stew!" Leaping out of bed, she tore towards the kitchen as Lizzy burst out laughing. A few seconds later, she heard Kate cursing softly.

Lizzy got up and followed Kate into the kitchen. "What?"

Kate looked at her in dismay, the smoking pot of stew in her hand. Her hair was tossed and wild, and her sexiness in that moment took Lizzy's breath away. Meanwhile, the stink of burnt lamb filled the air. "It's ruined," Kate said. "I'm so sorry."

Lizzy just laughed, and putting the pot back on the stove, she took Kate in her arms once again. "I'm not. I wanted to take you out to dinner anyway."

Kate pulled back and looked up at her. "Really? I thought you might be mad at me. You know...for leaving."

Lizzy kissed Kate's forehead. "God no."

Kate persisted curiously. She glanced up, continuing to study Lizzy. "Why not?"

Lizzy pushed a strand of strawberry blonde hair from Kate's face. "Because I love you. And because I understand you."

"Are you sure about that, Lizzy?"

"I guess I have a lot to learn about you, too. But I understand why you moved out."

Kate regarded her. "And why is that?"

"Because you needed space, like you said. We weren't ready yet. And I was just taking it personally, but now I'm not." Lizzy looked at Kate as she spoke, gently pushing her hair back in place, almost meditatively, piece by piece. More than ever, she was aware of a larger truth: she just wanted to be with Kate, wherever and however that might be.

"Turns out it wasn't about me after all," Lizzy said after a moment.

Kate smiled at her lover. "It's not. I'm glad you understand." Then she nodded to the bedroom. "Because what happens in there, that's the easy part, Lizzy. This right here…this is the hard part."

Lizzy nodded. "I know." She looked at Kate, standing there before her, her beautiful body naked in the kitchen twilight. She would never find another Kate, and now it was up to her to do the right thing with every choice she made.

Or when she made the wrong choice, to change course and make her amends.

"I have to tell you something else," Lizzy continued.

Kate nodded. "Go on."

Lizzy put her hands on her hips and looked out the kitchen window for a moment. This was going to be harder than she thought. "So look, Kate. There's something you should know about," she began.

Kate's gaze did not leave her own. "I'm listening." She folded her arms. Now Kate had a look of resigned patience on her face, and Lizzy realized she had no idea what she was about to say.

Lizzy took a deep breath. "So Mindy Rose has been threatening me and T, and you, and the garage."

Kate's eyes widened. "No! What? Why didn't you...?"

Lizzy held up a hand, silencing her. "Just listen, please." Kate set her jaw tensely, but she remained quiet. "Mindy says she's reported you to ICE and they'll be coming after you any day now. She's also threatening to shut down Driven because you worked for us."

Turning away, Kate threw her hands up in the air. "That woman is insane. I worked for *her* for seven years! As if..."

"Wait! Just listen to the rest of this, okay?" Lizzy stepped behind Kate, gently enfolded her in her arms. Holding her tight, she spoke directly into her ear.

"See the thing is, I've got you. Whether we're together or not, Kate. *I've got you.* Either way. You're not leaving this country. Not unless you want to." Lizzy took a breath, inhaling in this moment and all of its portent. Then she continued.

"Mindy doesn't know where you live now. All she really knows is that you might show up at Driven, so that's where she thinks ICE is going to bust you. But Tenika and I are getting a restraining order on her on Monday, for threatening our business. Then she can't come within 100 yards of Driven."

Kate pulled back and looked at her anxiously. "Really?"

"Yeah. Really."

Kate's posture relaxed slightly, and her arms hung by her side. Suddenly, she looked like a little girl who'd lost her mother in the grocery store. "And you're sure they can't find me?"

Lizzy shook her head. "How can they? It isn't even a legal sublet. Anyway, Mindy thinks you still live with me. So actually, it's pretty perfect that you moved out. At any rate, so as long as you stick around here, you should be okay. And who knows if ICE is even interested?"

Kate was quiet for a moment. "Thank you, Lizzy. Really. I appreciate it, I do." She looked up at her girlfriend, and then she sighed. "But I have to ask, darling. Why didn't you tell me sooner?"

Lizzy hung her head. "I'm sorry. I should have." She looked up at Kate with a pained expression. "I don't know. I guess I thought if I could be a hero, then you'd want me back."

"Lizzy!" Kate almost laughed out loud. "That is utterly mad. You know that, don't you?"

"Yeah," Lizzy said in a small voice.

Kate took Lizzy's face in her hands. "I want to be with you. I've told you this. I even want to live with you again when the time is right."

Lizzy looked at her somberly. "But?"

"But *nothing.*"

A smile broke across Lizzy's face. "Seriously?"

"Yes! Of course! Lizzy, I've been trying to tell you this all along, but you couldn't hear me! What's it going to...?"

Lizzy held up her hand, again, to stop the torrent of words coming out of Kate's mouth. "I know! I know! Okay, I get it. I..." Suddenly, Lizzy ran out of words. "Sally was trying to tell..." She looked at Kate and then she chuckled at herself. "Oh, forget it," Lizzy said, throwing up her hands. "Just come here, okay?"

Taking Kate in her arms, their tongues now found each other, moving into a deep long kiss. Then they both looked at each other happily, foreheads touching. "Feels like it's been a year," Lizzy said.

"It's been a week."

"Yeah." Now Lizzy rested her cheek easily against Kate's head. It felt so good, so right to be with her again. Every fiber in Lizzy's being was now finally relaxing.

Suddenly Kate turned to Lizzy and looked up at her. "And there's one more thing," she added slowly. "I love you."

Kate's words landed on Lizzy like a beautiful soft rain. Lizzy smiled shyly, as she slid ever deeper into surrender to her love. "Oh, honey," she said. "I love you, too."

"Oh! And one more thing!" Kate's face brightened. "Let's get the media."

"Get the media where?"

"You said there's a hearing, right? Get them to the hearing. Or I will, but I'll have to get on it immediately." Kate's eyes were lit with excitement. Breaking away from Lizzy, she began to pace around the kitchen, thinking aloud. "That will certainly help, but we might also add some other pieces."

Spinning around, Kate rambled on, her wheels fully engaged. She looked downright inspired. "Let's get a nice big crew of paparazzi to wait outside the courthouse for Mindy when she comes out. I can leak the story, and I know just where to do it. A few hits of national publicity...oh, that will do *nicely.*"

"Sounds perfect," Lizzy said. "You just tell me what you want me to do, honey, and I'm in."

Then she shook her head in admiration, watching her lover in motion. She was back.

They were back.

*

"Where are you taking me?" Delilah asked, sliding onto the worn passenger seat of Tenika's truck.

Tenika smiled at her, and then glancing over her shoulder, she began backing out of the driveway. "You'll see."

"Am I dressed all right?" Delilah smoothed out the vintage green and tan skirt she wore. It had a cowgirl theme, and it was one of her favorites.

Tenika chuckled as she put the truck into gear. "You look perfect, baby." Reaching over from the gear shift, she gave her lover's knee a squeeze. "You'll need a sweater or a jacket. You got one?"

"Yep. Why won't you tell me where we're going?" Delilah asked, and Tenika just shrugged.

"You know me, a woman of mystery."

Delilah rolled her eyes. "T, honey. I'm sorry, but you are so not a woman of mystery." This sudden plan of Tenika's had completely thrown her off, but she'd decided to just go with it. Delilah, of course, had had a plan of her own.

In her mind, it was all going to be perfect. As soon as Tenika got home from work, took a shower and changed, Delilah would whisk her into her car. Then eventually, after half an hour of sitting in the dregs of rush hour traffic, they'd arrive at Albany Bulb just in time for a glorious sunset over the San Francisco Bay.

They'd gone there on their first date. Then they would come back at key moments when they had to talk something through, or to celebrate an anniversary of one sort or another. It was their place, plain and simple.

Albany Bulb was a beach and a habitat, of sorts. It had gone from being a gathering place for great blue herons and egrets to being a dump pegged for landfill. When that closed, it became a homeless encampment, which eventually transformed into a homemade art park after the squatters were forced out.

The rough edges and wild creativity of rebar sprouting sculptures and graffiti gone crazy appealed to them both. Just beyond all of it was the ever-changing Bay. Silhouetted against a brilliant ocean sunset, a ten-foot-tall woman with outstretched scrap metal arms pled for something silent and unknowable. Her metal hair appeared to blow in a sea breeze. Her skirt, a flowing amalgam of found objects, scraps of tin, and even a few car parts, seemed to move as if she was alive. But mostly, she was just pleading.

Behind her, a shack was spray-painted to look like a rock wall. It was adorned with red and white serpentine graffiti, an artful blend of gang tagging, and something you might see in an alley in Oakland's Chinatown. Closer to the shore, a huge reclining creature, a cross between a cow and a gryphon, contemplated life with a sanguine look on its face. It was made entirely of driftwood, painstakingly pieced together in a supreme act of love.

As their truck pushed along 80, heading for the sunset and the Bulb, Delilah began to suspect they were on the same page. She glanced over at her lover. "So if you won't tell me where we're going, will you at least tell me why you wanted this date?"

"Why?" Tenika smiled at the highway unfurling in front of them. "What kind of question is that? Because I want to take you out. Isn't that reason enough? Have a little faith," she said.

"Okay." Delilah looked out the window at the passing pastiche of new construction along the highway. They were definitely going to the Bulb. She wondered what was up. Glancing into the backseat, she only saw the usual items stuffed into a canvas bag. The beach blanket. A bottle of cabernet and a few cups. There appeared to be nothing more than that.

Maybe it really was just a sunset date for no reason, she decided. Stranger things had happened. At any rate, Delilah would now be perfectly poised to read her poem to Tenika and tell her the news. It was a perfect place to share a little gratitude.

They arrived at the Bulb a few moments later, and Tenika grinned over at her. "Only a few minutes to sunset," she said.

Grabbing the bag in the back, Tenika slung it over her shoulder. Then walking to Delilah's side of the truck, she held out her hand. "Come on," she said. Hand in hand, they made their way down to the tiny park by the Bay.

Before them, the sunset was just slipping into high gear. Peach and pale blue filled the sky above a perfectly still, glassy bay, every bit of it reflecting the fantastic quilt of color above. In the center of the sky, a massive swath of rose and purple fanned out from the glowing slit of gold sun. The horizon, shrouded in a low-lying fog, was a soft, tea-smoked pink.

"Oh my God," Delilah said softly.

"Yep," said Tenika, finding a spot at the edge of the beach. She spread out the blanket. "Here," she said, patting the spot beside her. Wordless, Delilah slipped in next to her lover, and Tenika put her arm around her. Together, they watched silently.

After a moment, Tenika spoke. "This here," she said. "This is what I always wanted. A whole lot of it, at least," she said.

"Oh?"

"Mmm-hmm. I always wanted this life on the Bay. I always wanted the work I have and the garage. And I always wanted you." Shyly she turned to her partner. "I'm sorry," she said.

"T, honey…." Delilah searched her face. "What on earth are you apologizing for?"

"I just didn't realize how damn lucky I am. But I know now." Tenika's eyes returned to the horizon, which was now disappearing as the sunset deepened. "I learned a lot in the last week or so. Mostly, I learned you can't fight the river," she said.

Reaching into her pocket, Tenika produced a small dark velvet box. "Here," she said simply.

Immediately, Delilah froze. The box being handed to her appeared to have an engagement ring in it. She took it, and it felt almost weightless in her hand. *Assume nothing*, she cautioned herself. She took a deep breath. "Oh, T…baby…"

Tenika turned to her now with an intent look on her face. "Open it."

Slowly, almost painfully, Delilah lifted the lid on the small box, and there before her was a shimmering diamond Scottie on a gold band. She looked at Tenika, almost confused.

"Marry me, Delilah," Tenika said. "Then I really will have everything."

Delilah was scarcely able to talk. "Really? But you never wanted to get married."

"Yeah, that's what I always thought." Tenika looked out at the operatic sunset, climaxing before them. "Turns out I was wrong."

Delilah was silent, taking it all in.

Now Tenika glanced at her partner. "So what do you think?"

"Oh my God! Of course, I'll marry you. Of course!" Delilah threw her arms around her lover. Then she kissed her hard. "That's all I ever wanted, too."

"When it's right," Tenika began.

"It's right. And wait..." Tears were now running down Delilah's face, and she was both laughing and crying at the same time. "Wait!" she said, trying to get a grip. "Oh my God, I can't believe this."

"Well, yeah." Tenika smiled. "Believe it. I finally woke up."

Delilah took Tenika's arm. "No—you don't get it. Honey, I wanted to tell you this tonight. My MRI was normal. *Normal.* I don't have anything seriously wrong. *I'm okay!* It's just some kind of benign tremor. I called the doctor, and there are drugs I can take."

Now Tenika sat back. "Seriously?"

"Yes! I'm okay. We're okay!"

"Well, we were always okay. There was a little rough spot but..."

"You wanted to marry me anyway." Now Delilah looked at her partner with tears running down her face. "You didn't even know I was okay."

Tenika looked at her tenderly.

"Oh, baby." Leaning over, Delilah kissed her lover, now her fiancée. Then she pulled back. "I have something for you, too."

Tenika smiled. "Oh yeah?"

Unfolding a piece of paper from her pocket, Delilah looked out at the sunset, which was settling into a final orange-hued fade. A half-light had fallen over them, the pre-darkness dusk. "When I found out I was okay this afternoon, I realized how much you supported me. I just wanted to thank you. Actually, I was going to bring you out here as a surprise."

Tenika chuckled. "Guess this really is our place."

"Exactly." Clearing her throat now, Delilah began to read.

No matter what you do
Or what I do
Here's what I know
You are enough
And I am enough
And together, we are far more than enough

We have each other in sickness and in health
In good and bad
In stupidity and intelligence
In certainty and vagueness
In being right and being wrong
In all the absolutes of life
No matter who's watching
Or what's going on

We get through it
Just as we always will
Because we are enough
You and me
Just as we are
Total and absolute
Forever us

When she finally looked up, she saw that Tenika had her eyes closed. Tenika opened her eyes, and taking Delilah's hand, she kissed it. "It's perfect," she said. "Can I read it?"

Delilah handed over the sheet of paper, and silently, Tenika read it through.

"That is beautiful," Tenika said simply when she was finished. "And you wrote it for me?"

Delilah nodded. "For us. See, that's the funny thing. I had just decided it really was okay if we never got married."

Tenika shook her head. "Of course you did. That's what I mean when I say it's all perfect." Happily, she gazed at her lover. "So you going to try on the ring?"

"Oh, almost forgot." Taking the box in her hands, Delilah looked up and laughed. "I really can't believe any of this."

Now Delilah slipped the ring on her finger. "Perfect fit," she said, gazing at it happily. She turned to Tenika. "And it's a Scottie!"

"And you really like it? Because we can return it…"

Delilah put her hands to her chest protectively, guarding the ring. "No way in hell!"

Tenika laughed. "So that's a yes then?"

"That's a huge, emphatic, soaring, infinite HELL YES!" Delilah insisted.

They kissed as the last sliver of sunset slipped away.

Both of them had most definitely gotten what they came for.

Chapter Twenty

Lizzy sat on the brown wooden bench at the back of the courtroom, jiggling her foot. Beside her, Tenika was reviewing papers in a manila folder.

"Chill, please," Tenika said, casting an annoyed look in her business partner's direction.

Lizzy let out a long exhale and turned her head this way and that, loosening her neck. "Believe me, I'm trying."

Their appointment with the judge was due to begin any moment, but Mindy Rose still had not shown up. Which was no surprise.

By now, Tenika and Lizzy were fully prepared. They had a corroborating statement from a neighbor who watched Mindy lose it in front of Lizzy's house. More importantly, they'd also gotten a signed statement from Bernard, their landlord, verifying that Mindy had called him out of the blue and proposed forcing Driven out of their lease. She'd even provided a new tenant willing to pay market rates.

Even though he'd raised their rent several months earlier, Bernard had since come around. The higher rent still stood. But now, perhaps in an act of contrition, or perhaps because he'd been the landlord for Driven for years, he'd offered to come to the courthouse and testify on their behalf.

There was no doubt that their formerly friendly landlord was feeling guilty, which was just fine with Lizzy and Tenika. They now had enough evidence to at least state their case convincingly to the judge, which they would do whether or not the defendant bothered to show up.

A weary looking clerk stood up. "Calling Lizzy Edgewood, Tenika Stanford, and Mindy Rose Czernick." The judge, a middle-aged Asian man in a black robe, peered up. "Is the defendant here yet?"

Tenika and Lizzy stood up. "We haven't seen her yet, your honor," Tenika answered. There was a moment of quiet as the judge reviewed his docket of cases. Meanwhile, the clerk went outside into the hall. "Mindy Rose Czernick," they could hear him calling through the door.

Lizzy focused on the black and white sign posted on the wood paneled wall in front of her, trying to still her furiously beating heart. *No Cell Phones, No Pagers, No Food/Gum, No Drinks.*

A fluorescent hum from the overhead lights was the only audible sound in the room as a few dozen Oakland residents waited quietly for their turn with the judge. The mood in the place was weary and flat, as if every last person was exhausted by the sheer stress of whatever had brought them there.

Suddenly the door swept open, and Mindy entered in a perfume-scented whoosh. She was wearing a dark suit and a hot pink satin blouse, along with bright red stilettos and a large pair of sunglasses. Behind her, a female attorney with frosted hair and a loaded briefcase struggled to keep up.

"Alright, everyone," Mindy declared, with the air of a woman used to commanding a room. "I'm here. Let's get on with it, shall we?" Her gaze pivoted from left to right and back again quickly. Pointedly, she ignored Tenika and Lizzy. "Where shall I sit?" she asked the judge loudly.

The attorney pointed out a chair to the left, and she seated herself in front of the judge. "I'm representing Miss Czernick, and..." she began.

"You can direct all questions to me," Mindy blurted. The attorney shot her a sharp look, and then shuffled the raft of notes in front of her.

The court clerk interrupted them. "Plaintiffs, please rise." Lizzy and Tenika dutifully stood up. "Parties will remain standing and raise your right hand," she began for the seventh time that morning. "Do you solemnly under penalty of perjury swear to tell the whole truth…"

A moment later all were sworn in, and the judge began his statement. "In the matter now pending before the court, there is a request for a restraining order against defendant Mindy Czernick." The judge looked directly at Tenika and Lizzy. "The question, plaintiffs, is if you can prove through a preponderance of evidence that such an order is merited."

Lizzy swallowed hard. "Well, judge—your Honor, uh."

"We have it right here," offered Tenika. "I have a lot of documents for you, your Honor. Everything I previously submitted." Neatly she produced her file, and a moment later handed it over to the clerk who then handed it to the judge. Silence ensued as the judge reviewed the documents.

"Excuse me, your Honor," Mindy's attorney looked mildly alarmed. "I believe we…"

He waved for her to be silent. "This will be sufficient," he said to Tenika. Then he turned to Mindy Rose. "Ms. Czernick, why are you harassing these women and trying to close their business?"

"If I may, your Honor," the attorney began, but Mindy now interrupted her.

"What on earth makes you think I'm trying to close their garage?" she asked. Mindy's voice now turned up at the end of the question as if it were the most preposterous idea in the world.

The judge just looked at her. "The neighbors heard you screaming that you're going to close down their business. What were you thinking?"

Now Mindy grew haughty. "I never did such a thing," she protested.

"Your Honor," her attorney began futilely once more. But all hope was already lost.

The judge looked nonplussed. "I have a signed statement from a witness who saw the entire incident at Miss Edgewood's home, Miss Czernick, and another from the landlord for the Driven Garage saying you tried to enlist him to drive them out of business. You are therefore being ordered to stay away from the Driven Garage and the homes of its owners for the next three years." His gavel came down. "Case closed."

In a flash, Mindy was on her feet. "Now wait a minute here!" she demanded. "This is a sham! You have no right to..."

"Case closed," the judge repeated more loudly. Then he nodded to the clerk who attempted to escort Mindy to the door. "Get off of me!" she protested as he took her arm.

The attorney leaned in and whispered something to Mindy that made her recoil. "Fuck off, you idiot!" she spat as Lizzy and Tenika watched spellbound. Furiously, she turned on her heel and strode out of the courtroom.

A moment later, as they all moved down the industrial-looking hallway in Mindy's wake, she became even more explosive. But this time, as she stepped through the doors of the courthouse, she was red faced, furious, and ranting to whomever would listen. Meanwhile, a sudden host of reporters with microphones leaned in to get her remarks on record as photographers jostled for a better angle.

At least twenty paparazzi had shown up to document Mindy's meltdown. "Get away from me!" she screamed, as she pushed and shoved at the offending members of the media. Meanwhile, her attorney kept trying to attract their attention. "Mindy Rose has done nothing wrong!" she said to no one because no one was listening.

Instead, the cameras and the microphones followed the now fleeing Mindy down the street as Lizzy shot picture after picture of the scene. One stray news reporter standing outside a KRON-4 truck stopped Tenika as she and Lizzy passed by. "Do you have any comments?"

"It's a great day for democracy, and for the Driven Garage," Tenika said.

"Woman-owned, and woman-powered," Lizzy added.

"Yeah, we're not going anywhere but up." Tenika beamed. "Y'all stop by now," she said, looking directly at the camera.

"Drop by to chat in our conversation corner," Lizzy threw in. "We'd love to get to know you!" She'd promised Kate she would add that part.

Kate.

In thirty seconds, she'd be sharing her pictures of Mindy fleeing the media, for immediate release. And the news that the order was in place, and that Kate was safe for now. ICE would be unlikely to find Kate in her current hideaway. Mindy, meanwhile, had disappeared.

"Great work," Lizzy said to her business partner. She patted her shoulder. "You and Kate totally had that dialed in."

Tenika paused. "You've got to hang on to that girl, sister. She's a keeper."

Lizzy nodded. "Oh, I am. Believe me. She can live in that apartment on her own as long as she wants. I'm done trying to micromanage this thing."

Tenika smiled. "Way to go."

A moment later Lizzy texted the photos to Kate, who instantly shot back a reply.

"AMAZING!" was all it said. Lizzy smiled.

As Lizzy sat in the momentary stillness of Tenika's truck, she thanked God and anyone else who might be listening for the chance to solve the problem at hand. And for the chance to be Kate's lover once again.

She and Kate would prevail. She knew it. There would be another chapter for sure.

*

Sally lay in bed on Tenika and Delilah's couch and watched head-lights move across the ceiling. She was too wired to sleep, but too sleepy to stay upright for one more moment.

The problem was Frankie.

Sally had just spent the last 90 minutes talking to Frankie, running up one conversation avenue and down the next in a phone call she had only half expected to get. She'd hung up in a haze of lust, excitement, and sheer connection. Honestly, she never thought they'd get here.

But then that was just like life, wasn't it?

One minute you were praying to the Mother Goddess for some kind of deliverance after your shitty break up. Then less than a month later, you were having a ribald flirt with an incredibly sexy police officer. A cop, of all people. Neatly, Sally tucked away her feelings about people who used weapons and moved on with her thoughts.

Rolling over, she checked in with herself. How was she feeling about things at this exact moment? The answer came up quickly. She was feeling hot, hopeful. And completely alive.

Frankie would be more than just girlfriend number thirteen. Just like Sally, she was here to transform and be transformed. To surrender to the great web of love that held them all, and healed them all. And by doing so, Frankie would become just another piece of the infinite puzzle that was Sally's life.

It was all fated. And it was all perfect.

Reaching over to the coffee table, Sally pulled open her box of Goddess cards. Mixing up the well-worn golden deck on her stomach, she gave it an extra shuffle as she considered the prospect of being Frankie's lover. Then she pulled a card. Not surprisingly, a second card jumped out at her, as well.

Sally turned over the first card. It was Kwan Yin, the Goddess of Compassion. Immediately, Sally understood why this card had surfaced, for Frankie was clearly in need of an understanding shoulder to lean against. She might be a cop, but her heart and her soul were just as vulnerable as everyone else's.

Yet, Sally needed to give herself a little compassion as well. As intense and interesting as Frankie might seem to her in this moment, she needed to proceed with care. Only recently her heart had been completely under siege. Sally tucked this inconvenient thought away, uncertain if she even wanted to remember it.

Then she turned over the second card. As ever, yet again, it was Bast, the Goddess of Independence. This time, Bast was in the upright position. Sally smiled.

Somehow, she'd turned a corner in the last week. She'd come to terms with her own flailing, and had dropped an anchor back into the flow of life again. She could see just how things were going to go.

She would move out soon and find her own place. She would finally begin her business and become a legitimate psychic.

She would make choice after choice, and pretty soon her bank account would be full again. Just like her heart, her soul, and the rest of her life.

Sally understood the truth now. Each day was just another precious chance to compose the picture and get it right.

She couldn't wait to get started.

About Suzanne Falter

Suzanne Falter is an author, speaker, blogger and podcaster who has published both fiction and non-fiction, as well as essays. Her queer fiction titles include the funny romantic suspense series Transformed. She also writes and speaks about self-care and the transformational healing of crisis, especially in her own life after the death of her daughter Teal. Her non-fiction books include *How Much Joy Can You Stand?*, *Living Your Joy*, and *Surrendering to Joy*. Suzanne's essays have appeared in *O Magazine*, *The New York Times*, *Elephant Journal*, and *Thrive Global* among others. Suzanne is also the host of podcasts The Self-Care Soother and Before the Afterlife. Her free flash fiction can be found at suzannefalterfiction.com, as well as on Facebook, Twitter, YouTube, and Pinterest. She lives with her wife in the San Francisco Bay Area.

Also by Suzanne Falter

Fiction
Oaktown Girls series
Driven
Committed
Destined
Revealed

Transformed: San Francisco
Transformed: Paris
Transformed: POTUS
(All titles by Suzanne Falter & Jack Harvey)

Non-Fiction
The Extremely Busy Woman's Guide to Self-Care
The Joy of Letting Go
Surrendering to Joy
How Much Joy Can You Stand?
Living Your Joy

Many thanks to the following people for their help with the development and writing of this book:

I got enormous help from TW, Diving Swallow Tattoo, several judges from Hayward and Wiley E. Manuel Courthouses, and Grandma's Garage.

Thank you to my wonderful wife for her edit, inspiration, encouragement and legal system guidance.

As ever a joy to work with my production team, Danielle Hartman Acee, Lynn Bosworth and Carolyn Manchoulis.

And thanks, most of all, to Jack Harvey.